ATLAS FORMAN
&
THE NECESSARY DREAM

Written By Derek Holser

Printed in the United States of America.

Special thanks to Leah Holser, Samantha Blackmer, David Burnett, Sara Norcott, Anna Keane, Esther Keane, The Hinz Family, & Frankie Franklin.

Design by Ross Fitzgerald, Beyond Creative™

ISBN 978-0-9882805-4-0

0 9 8 8 2 8 0 5 4 X

Because life is much more than we can see.

It's what we say.

David Hall

For Mom.
You always liked this story the best.

CHAPTER 1

They say parents should never have to bury a child. But that's what Mom and Dad were about to do the late May morning I began to discover that daydreams were more than mere fantasy; the day I discovered life is not just what we see. It's what we say.

Hannah and me were riding in the back of Meemaw's bright blue sedan, near the front of the funeral procession. Everyone in town was trailing behind us. If misery were a hotel, it was a no vacancy kind of day.

We were third in the caravan of cars, led by a black and silver hearse carrying the body of Charlie Forman, hometown football hero and my big brother.

Mom was ahead of us, driving the station wagon. Dad

was ahead of her, just behind the hearse, driving his freshly polished Corvette. The car I was never allowed to sit in, even after Charlie was gone. Or maybe especially now that Charlie was gone. I guess Mom and Dad didn't want to share that ride with anyone, even each other.

My suit was too small. I'd last worn it for sixth grade graduation. My socks showed when I walked. Seventh grade had been full of growth. My body increased in height and my face increased in zits.

The formal outfit was annoying but I was glad to be wearing pants; otherwise my legs would be sticking to the vinyl cover on the bench seat in the back of Meemaw's car.

"Atlas? Why did the drunk man crash into Charlie?" Hannah's barely-there voice asked from the seat beside me. I glanced over at her, bit my lip, and blinked fast to squelch the tears. In spite of the ache in my heart, I couldn't help marveling at her tender confusion. She was a sweet little bundle of innocence.

Mom had curled Hannah's red hair into spirals that hung around her freckled face. Her light green eyes were tinged pink from days of crying. Mom made sure Hannah got a new outfit, a light blue and pale yellow plaid dress. She looked like one of the porcelain dolls Meemaw had in her spare bedroom, the room with dusty ceiling fan and the painted wicker furniture. I glanced above the neat bow in Hannah's hair and saw a puff of white tissue rising from the gingham-checked crocheted tissue box in the back window.

"Why Atlas? Why?" Hannah insisted.

"M-m-mom s-s-s-says he w-w-wasn't..." I stopped talking and clenched my fists. Stupid stutter. Like a tomcat with a dead rodent, it toyed with my tongue. Always lingering, ready to pounce and make a mockery of my words with ridiculous sounds.

"It's ok, Atlas." Meemaw's low gravelly voice, produced by her faithful inhalation of two packs a day since she was seventeen, interjected. The stress of the funeral caused her to break her rule about smoking around us kids. She puffed away as we drove toward the cemetery.

Her window was cracked, drawing out the smoke as we drove along. The passing breeze had no chance at sucking away her car's ever-present stale smoke odor. Not that she noticed; Meemaw wore that bowling-alley aroma like a second skin.

"Don't talk now, Atlas. Hannah, dear, sometimes bad things happen." She turned up her hillbilly music a little louder and whispered to herself, "Seems to me most of the bad things happen to the really good people."

I guess she thought we couldn't hear her. But we could. It's surprising how often grown-ups think kids aren't listening. We're always listening.

We reached the T-intersection that marked the edge of the civilized part of Pinesburg, Kentucky. Our family home for four generations, Pinesburg is a hick town surrounded by hick towns in coal country, near the West

Virginia border.

Meemaw turned right, barely two breaths behind Mom's car. The repetitive click of the hazard lights produced a mechanical backbeat to the squalling fiddles playing in the speaker behind my ear.

We were just a mile or so from the cemetery. Meemaw squished her cigarette butt into the plastic tray her third husband Marty had velcroed to the top of the dashboard. About three years earlier, Marty had been buried in the same cemetery we were now approaching.

Marty was a clever guy and a lot more fun than Meemaw's first husband, my mom's dad. But no one called him Grandpa. Mom wouldn't allow it. I remember her saying often, "You have one Grandfather, and he's in Heaven. You better believe this man, Marty, is nothing like your grandfather."

Meemaw cleared her throat and added, for Hannah's benefit, "We can't understand everything in this life. You'll come to find out that's the truth more often than not. Charlie is in heaven now. And when you're really old and go to heaven, you'll get to see him again."

Hannah looked down at her shiny black patent leather shoes. She pushed her stubby fingers against the clear plastic between her chunky thighs and the seat.

"Daddy says you're older than coal, Meemaw. Does that mean you'll get to see Charlie first?"

I snickered. Then I laughed out loud. I looked in the

rear view mirror at Meemaw's tired eyes and raisin-skinned lips. They began to stretch into a grin.

"Your daddy says I'm older than coal, eh? Well he is…" Meemaw smiled as she caught her tongue.

"Yes, Hannah, I suppose so." Then she laughed. It was unexpected, but she kept laughing while crying. Then she started coughing hard like she was choking.

"Meemaw!" I shouted. "Are you ok?"

She gasped several times and finally stopped coughing.

"I'm fine, Atlas. Hand me those tissues." She waved her nicotine-stained, turquoise-ringed hand at the back window.

I reached over Hannah's head and as I did, I looked out the back window. Cigarette smoke drifted up from the open windows of the cars behind us, giving the impression of dozens of portable miniature chimneys. I guess everyone was breaking their rule about smoking around the kids today.

I grabbed the stiff plastic tissue box and paused, pulling out a clump of tissues for Hannah and me. I handed the box to Meemaw.

"Thank you," Meemaw said.

Her chest rattled as she reached for the depths with a lung-clearing cough. She hacked up the obstructing gunk, gushed it into the wad of tissue and tucked the whole mess into her purse. Two minutes later, we were parked next to

mom's wagon at the foot of the hillside where Charlie was
to be buried.

CHAPTER 2

Mom was standing in front of her car, waiting for
us to get out of Meemaw's car. Mom's face was puffy and
her nose was runny yet she still looked pretty. Her bobbed
auburn hair accented her pale slender neck. Through
the tears, her glistening blue eyes kept a quiet strength,
matched by the physical strength of a petite frame that had
competed in many a triathlon over the years.

I stuffed the tissues into my suit coat pocket and
tugged on the door handle.

"I'll get Hannah," Meemaw said as she lurched out
from under the cracked plastic oversized steering wheel,
"but first, straighten your hair and your tie."

I looked at my reflection in the car window. My

familiar gangly body, capped by my long narrow face and lopsided ears, looked back. Dark circles hung below deep-set hazel eyes. A handful of strands of dark hair stood straight up at the front of my part. A fresh trail of zits streaked across my forehead like a constellation of pink stars.

Straightening my hair is the least of my concerns, I thought.

I pressed down as hard as I could, holding my hair in place for the moment.

"That looks better," Meemaw said.

Mom silently walked toward me, her trembling arms extended. A silver monogram pendant flashed in the sunlight as it dangled from her neck. Charlie and I had given it to her for Mother's Day, less than two weeks ago.

The gravity of her grief sucked me into a bear hug before I could say a word. I think she mumbled, "I love you," but I couldn't be certain. She was just a bundle of blubbering gasps and gurgles.

Mom's grip squeezed the façade of calm right off me. I couldn't fight it anymore. First, a couple of watery dribbles trickled out of the corner of my eye. Then, a flood. We rained tears onto each other's shoulders and stared through the hurt at the cracked asphalt beneath our feet. As I wept, my nose filled with that dirty paper smell of a cigarette being lit. Meemaw was standing just behind us holding Hannah's tiny hand, but in that moment, everyone else seemed miles away. Especially Dad.

I stepped back from Mom and as I wiped at my face with the tissue, I looked at Dad standing halfway up the hillside, like a soldier, itching for his orders. Dad never waited for anyone. He called it being a leader. I call it being inconsiderate.

"Atlas?" a tiny voice behind me whispered.

I felt Hannah's fingers brush my thigh, then grab the hem of my suit jacket. I looked down at her and sniffled. I couldn't look her in the eye or the waterworks would pour once more. I silently gripped her hand. Our sweaty palms pressed together like an envelope being sealed, locking us together for the dreaded climb up the hill to Charlie's grave.

As we slowly walked through the overgrown grass, I looked over my shoulder and saw Wyatt Jamison, my one true friend. As usual, his blonde hair was parted on the side and slicked down tight against his head, except for the cowlick in the front corner of his part. His athletic frame was swallowed whole by his older brother's tent of a hand-me-down sport coat.

"I'm real sorry Atlas, everyone's real tore up about Charlie," Wyatt whispered as he approached.

"Thanks Wyatt," I replied, turning my head down.

Wyatt picked up on my let's-not-talk vibe, and contrary to his nature, complied.

Through the checkerboard pattern of crumbling brick-sized grave markers we walked, careful not to step on

13

them. The dates were old and nearly worn away but not a single one memorialized an adult. Most were infants and toddlers. All of us locals knew the story about this patch of graves. I had heard since I was a boy about how our town almost disappeared over one hundred years earlier.

In 1883, Pinesburg nearly got wiped out by the consumption. That's what the old folks called tuberculosis. More than half the kids died and most of the parents wished they'd had. Pinesburg dwindled down to less than a hundred people. Just when the townsfolk were considering abandoning the whole place – there was just too much dark, everywhere – hope returned. The spread of the disease stopped. Literally, they say, a line could be drawn down the backside of the street where I live. From that line out, no one got sick anymore.

Some of the old-timers say there were guardian angels that showed up to end the suffering. Others talk about healing spirits that live in the hills all around our valley. A few even tell about mysterious lights in the sky and life returning to Pinesburg anew. Most everyone agreed that something supernatural happened.

Something natural happened around the same time, as well. Speculators found a huge vein of that black rock in the hills. Coal. They mined it and the money started pouring in, bringing new people with brighter memories than the locals and most important, brighter vision for the future. Ancient animal life, now a fuel for the factories up north and heat for the homes all around the hills, brought new life to Pinesburg.

I held Hannah's hand tighter as we reached the top of the hill. Mom and Dad and Meemaw walked under the corner of the green cloth awning stretched over the hole in the ground. Charlie's coffin, a black steel box with silver metal handles, was suspended over the hole with dark nylon straps.

The sight of it stopped me in my tracks. My parents and Meemaw kept walking. They didn't look at it. They couldn't look at it. My grip on Hannah loosened and she ran to the space between Mom and Meemaw. The three of them kept walking until they took their seats in the front row of plastic folding chairs on the other side of the open grave.

Wyatt stood beside me as I stared at the gleaming metal coffin. It was hard to accept Charlie was gone. Unexpected tragedy always is. I closed my eyes and thought about Charlie. The last time I saw him, in the intensive care unit in Louisville, he was all coiled up in tubes and wires like he was in a plastic snake pit.

I blinked a couple times and squeezed my eyes tight. I wished those healing spirits that saved Pinesburg had been around to save Charlie. Or taken me.

As I stood there, eyes closed, my hand reached out for the cold edge of Charlie's metal box. My heart raced. My desire to escape intensified. A cluster of bright yellow spots

15

danced across the inside of my eyelids and appeared in the space around my head.

"Just follow us," a chorus of high-pitched voices whispered.

A rush of wind blew through my hair.

So much for keeping it looking nice. Sorry, Meemaw.

"Can you fly?" The high-pitched voices asked.

"No," I replied.

The spots of light flashed across the ground, zoomed up into the awning overhead and came rushing back toward me. The bright spots combined into a cyclone of light just before colliding with my pimple-dotted forehead.

I staggered backward as it spun before me, banging into Charlie's coffin. As I tried to steady myself, I grabbed at his Pinesburg Wildcats football jersey, messing up the arrangement. The large flower wreath spread across the lower end of the coffin loosened and slid toward the ground.

"Atlas, Atlas," a voice whispered. The high-pitched chorus was gone. The dots of light were gone.

"Atlas." Wyatt was still beside me, whispering my name.

He tilted his head and arched his eyebrows, motioning for me to look across the coffin. My family was staring at me. Dad's eyes were so large and bugged it looked like a crawdad was stuck behind them trying to get out. Clearly, nearly knocking everything over next to my brother's coffin was not the proper thing to do. Another daydream, causing me nothing but trouble.

I dodged Dad's angry stare and looked at the crowd quietly moving into the rows behind him. Nods of hello and grimaces of sorrow filled the faces. Hushed voices of sadness filled the air.

As I walked to take my seat in the empty folding chair between Hannah and Meemaw, a glimmer of red light from beyond the rows of somber attendees flashed through the air. I would say it flashed through the sky, but it was pretty close to the ground. As I paused to look, the red light pulsed through the air a second time.

"Reckon I'll see you after," Wyatt whispered and walked off to join his family.

I didn't reply. I was trying to locate the source of the strange red glow and moved closer to the front row while scanning the space behind the last row of seats. In hindsight, I'm pretty lucky I didn't trip over something. That would have been typical.

"Get to your seat and quit your infernal daydreaming," Dad growled as I walked between him and the coffin.

"Leave him be," Mom replied. "His brother's dead, for God's sake." She started crying again and buried her face in a burgundy and black swirl-patterned scarf.

As I sat down Mom rubbed my arm, trying to comfort me from Dad's correction. Or maybe trying to comfort herself. I half-grinned at her, which only caused her to wail more loudly.

"It's ok, Mom," I whispered and slid my fingers inside her black-gloved hand. Even though it was closing in on summer, my insides felt like it was the dead of winter. As Mom shivered next to me, more from heartache than lack of heat, I wondered if I'd ever stop hearing voices and seeing things that weren't really there.

CHAPTER 3

"It is an inexplicable tragedy. The passing of the young." A nasal-intoned baritone announced from the other side of the coffin. I glanced over as it continued.

"We can never be sure why these things happen but we can be sure that God has the dearly departed in His loving arms…"

It was Brother Westler, the pastor from First Baptist. I couldn't look at him without recalling what Marty said every time Meemaw dragged him to church:

"That fat preacher ain't much to look at, and he sweats like a bunch of bananas in a plastic bag, but he's gonna durn sure scare the devil out of us and make sure we's all born again by the end of this service."

He'll probably try to make sure we's all born again, even at a funeral.

Especially at a funeral, I thought.

"One never knows when their time will come…" Brother Westler continued. Marty was right, this pastor was not an easy listen. There had to be something better to hold my attention until he was done talking. I turned my head and looked past Mom's shoulders, and out over the crowd.

As I looked beyond many familiar faces, all trying to avoid eye contact as fervently as I was, I felt one pair of eyes that refused to look away.

I vaguely recognized the moist feminine eyes tracking my movement. As soon as I saw the dark hair that hung long and silky around her face and shoulders, I knew without a doubt. I had been staring at that shimmering hair every Tuesday and Thursday afternoon in History class all year long. Like a black waterfall of temptation, it often splashed onto the front corner of my desktop. The dark hair and those moist eyes belonged to Aamilah Shamad, the cutest girl in school, at least in my rankings. One glance from her usually turned my face seven shades of red and tied my tummy up tighter than a guitar string one strum before it breaks.

Now she was sitting behind me. Way behind me, but directly in my line of sight. She was sitting in the back row, next to her mother, who was all wrapped up in a black robe dress. I don't know what they call those outfits, but it's what her mother wears every day. At least, I've never seen her without it. Aamilah's dad is a doctor, and they moved to Pinesburg from Egypt just a few months ago, just before we started seventh grade.

At least ten seconds passed and she held her stare like she was afraid I'd disappear if she blinked. I couldn't take it anymore. I abandoned my mission to avoid listening to Brother Westler and turned back around in my chair with the unmistakable impression that her eyes were still peering at the back of my head.

Is my cowlick popped up again? I wondered.

I slid my hand over the back of my head. As I did, I could feel those squirrely strands poking into the air like an airplane tower with the blinking red lights. I pushed them flat in futility, knowing they would jump to attention the moment I returned my hand to my lap.

"Charlie was like no one else. He was a wonderful son…"

Dad was speaking. He stood, tall and shiny, facing the crowd. His trademark smile was reduced to a resolved grin. His blue eyes danced like wave tops crashing against the shore and his perfectly parted salt and pepper hair capped his tanned face. He looked like a department store catalog model. He couldn't stop being handsome, even while grieving over the loss of my big brother.

"I'll never forget the time Charlie came home from school, upset because some of the other kids were picking

21

on a handicapped girl. Charlie stood up for the things that matter most. Ya'll know what I mean. He was all that's good about this world – and he did all that he could to stop the bad. He was a Pinesburg kind of boy."

The crowd nodded in unison.

Mom sobbed and sputtered into her silk scarf.

"That's right, Preston." A voice whispered from a few rows back.

I couldn't tell if Dad was mourning Charlie or running for mayor. A little of both, I guess. Ever since Dad's dad – the grandpa I never met – died as a hero in Vietnam, it was like Dad was trying to prove himself worthy of that legacy.

It was impossible for Dad to separate his ambition from his actions. If an occasion called for a speech, C. Preston Forman, III, Esq. was at the top of the list. Actually, in Pinesburg, he was the list.

"The Lord giveth and the Lord taketh, as was said by the prophet Job. We can not comprehend the ways of God." Dad finished with Scripture even though he hadn't seen the inside of the church since Christmas.

As Dad sat down, a satisfied tightness crept across his lips. The rustle of someone standing in the middle of the crowd interrupted the moment's silence. The unmistakable crinkling of unfolding paper followed.

"What's that?" an elderly lady whisper-shouted to her nearly deaf husband a few rows behind me.

22

Everyone turned to look.

A lanky man with graying temples and thick glasses stood in the middle of the seated mourners. His close-trimmed neck beard reminded me of a leprechaun. He was far too tall to be a leprechaun, though. He held a piece of paper in his hand and didn't look up.

I hooked my elbow behind Mom's chair and craned my neck to study the unknown eulogizer. He looked the part of the unexpected mourner, with a faint layer of dust atop the shoulders of his dark double-breasted suit. He likely wore his suit less frequently than me. His tie was a milky and lavender striped number, and his pale hands nearly blended in with the paper in his palm. Clearly an outsider, he looked nothing like Pinesburg's mostly blue-collar citizenry.

"Noble is the son who gains respect as he dies. Nobler still is the son who earns respect as he lives." The man's voice pierced the silence, crisp and clear as the morning air during deer season. It reminded me of the whistle of Wyatt's crossbow arrow before it thwacked into the side of his first kill last November. He forced me to go hunting with him, because that's what best friends are for. It was all right, but I'll never forget the way that deer yelped and trembled before it died.

As the strange man continued speaking, the crowd looked as stunned as that deer before it collapsed in the mud.

"The death of one lingers in the mind and heart longer than the death of thousands. But better, far better, is the loss of one than that the whole of the people perish. Though you struggled to find your compass on Earth, your Atlas remains for the good of us all. Rest in peace, Charles."

Dad stood and glared at the man, whose gaze never left the ground. The man stepped into the aisle and started to limp away. His hobble was so exaggerated it must have been for show. He practically dragged his right leg as he exited the audience, lamely staggering into the open field beyond the folding chairs without another word.

Unlike Wyatt's eight-point buck in November, the audience was able to shake off the daze of the dramatic stranger's pronouncement. It took a little longer for me, which might explain what happened next.

Brother Westler regained his composure by clearing his early stage emphysema lungs. The rattling phlegm chamber that was his chest caused half the people to sit up like soldiers.

"Is there anyone else who'd like to share a testimony about Charlie?" he asked. My hand and body shot up before I could stop myself.

"Yes, Atlas?"

Brother Westler looked as stunned as I felt. His perpetually judgmental brow furrowed deeper than the trench Charlie was about to enter.

What was I doing standing up? I didn't speak. I never

spoke. I couldn't speak.

"I r-r-r-rem-em-em—em-", I couldn't get the words out. "I-I-I-". Come on Atlas, spit it out. I clenched my fists and jammed them in my pockets. My forehead beaded with sweat and my heart raced like the starving greyhounds at Marty's favorite dog track. "I r-r-r-remember Charlie's sm-sm-smile."

As I slid backward into my seat, I saw that red glimmer again. This time, its reflection appeared in the silver trim on Charlie's coffin. I turned half around in my chair and looked back.

Just beyond Aamilah in the back row, a large willow tree stood alone. It seemed out of place. Maybe it was because there were no other trees within several hundred yards. It wasn't just alone; it seemed lonely. Its branches drooped with disappointment, like a beagle's ears. As I looked one last time, half of the tree shook like they do when a big thunder boomer is coming and the hot air gets pushed up and the cold wind blows. But there wasn't any wind. A second later, the red glimmer shot up from the trunk through a few branches, and out of the leaves into the air.

Other than the red streak of light, the sky appeared typical. Just a few clumps of marshmallows suspended in the eternal light blue veil above.

Hearing voices. Seeing lights. Are my daydreams getting stronger? Or is this really real?

CHAPTER 4

"Atlas, it's time to get going," Meemaw nearly shouted as she tugged on my sleeve.

I looked down. Charlie's coffin was in the ground. A tightly stretched black cloth lay over the hole. I guessed the dirt filler-inners would show up later.

I don't know how much time passed after I stammered about Charlie's smile, or if anyone else spoke. I couldn't stop wondering about the tree and the red glow. It didn't seem as though anyone else noticed it. Maybe it was just for me? Maybe it was welcoming my brother to the cemetery? I didn't know but I didn't feel afraid, which was strange. Usually the things we are most frightened by are the things we don't understand.

I stood up and looked back. The tree towered above the green turf, its whitish gray trunk and bark-covered veins twisting and turning out to their narrow green leaves. It was easy to see now because everyone was gone. No Wyatt. No Aamilah. No one. No red light, either.

I lingered a moment even though Meemaw was upset. We had to get home for the post-funeral potluck fellowship. That's what they call it when all the people from the community show their compassion by invading our house with mismatched Tupperware and old Cool Whip tubs stuffed with food no one wants to eat.

"Atlas, are you daydreaming again?"

The voice was coming from down the hill. It was Meemaw.

"Come on Atlas. Your Mother is going to want to have you and Hannah close by today. And for a long time to come."

She spoke with the wisdom of someone who'd buried three husbands, two sons, and now, a grandson.

"Yes ma'am," I hollered and started sprinting down the hillside, almost tumbling. I kept my feet and made it to Meemaw and Hannah.

"Come on now," she said, waving her arms and corralling us like a mother hen at nightfall. We had barely crossed from grass to asphalt when a thought entered my mind from our conversation just before we got to the cemetery.

"Meemaw?" I asked, slightly breathless.

"Yes, Atlas?" Meemaw replied.

"You *really think* Charlie is in Heaven? You *really think* there is a Heaven?"

Before she could answer, Hannah piped up. "At Sunday school, Miss Whitney says that all kids go to heaven. Except the ones who don't share."

Meemaw rubbed Hannah's little head. In one motion, she opened the passenger side rear door and slid Hannah onto the vinyl seat.

"That's a good answer, dear." Meemaw leaned in and clipped the seatbelt around Hannah's midsection.

I stood beside Meemaw as she huffed to push herself back to standing. I sniffed the air. Something about her extra-heavy perfume was, for once, comforting.

She shut Hannah's door and looked at me. "Why are you standing here, boy? Go on, get in the car."

I walked around the front of the car, drumming my fingers across its heavy metal hood. Meemaw went around the trunk end. We met in the middle and I opened the driver door.

"I was serious about Charlie and Heaven." I said as I held the heavy door open while Meemaw slipped behind the wheel.

She jammed the key into the ignition switch and just before starting the car, looked at me. Her rouge-laden bulbous cheeks reminded me of the nutcracker figures

Mom put out on the front porch every Christmas. Her leaky left eye twitched but her stare was as clear and bright as the freshly polished pendant hanging around her neck.

"I can promise you he's not in the other place," Meemaw finally answered. She emphasized her opinion by turning the key and revving the engine. "Now, get in the car. Your mom's already going to pitch a fit, us getting home so late." She tugged the door shut, and I jumped in my spot behind her.

We cruised home to the crowd of sympathizers and their mushy green bean casseroles. Meemaw was right, as usual. As people milled about, whispering with each other and avoiding eye contact with us, Mom sat on the good sofa and held Hannah in her lap. She made me sit beside them in the stiff velvet armchair the entire afternoon.

Wyatt, ever the good friend, sat beside me in a plastic folding chair. We mostly looked at the faded wooden floor as it disappeared beneath the fringe of the rug beneath our feet.

"Check this out," Wyatt said, after about ten minutes of nothing. He pulled a fist-sized rock from the inside pocket of his second-hand sport coat. It sparkled in the sunlight shining through the window over our shoulders. It was gray with purplish streaks, canary yellow specks and swirls the color of cinnamon.

"Wow, that's cool. Where'd you get it?" I asked.

"Down at our hideout, in the back of the cave."

Our hideout was actually an abandoned former staging spot for the coal miners. It hadn't been used in years. It wasn't far from my house, in the woods behind our street, just beyond the line where the tuberculosis miraculously stopped over one hundred years earlier.

Wyatt and I discovered it when we were seven or eight years old. It was mostly filled in, and the entrance was overgrown and nearly invisible, but there was a good room-sized space under the ground. It was a great place to hang out and plan summertime adventures.

"Man, I haven't been there in a while," I whispered.

"Yeah, we should clean it up and put in some string lights. We could do some neat stuff in there, make it like a home away from home," Wyatt replied. "Speaking of which, I saw some home-baked pies on the table. I'm kind of hungry." Wyatt rubbed his stomach.

"Go get some," I said, "I think I'm stuck here for the afternoon." I looked over at Mom, who was dabbing her eyes with tissue.

"All right, I will. I'm going to head home soon, ok?"

"Sure. I'll see you at school," I replied.

Wyatt tucked the rock back in his pocket and walked away, leaving me to mumble "thank you" to the remaining well-wishers as they streamed by our spot the rest of the afternoon.

When the last non-relative left, I looked at Mom. She held Hannah tighter than the waistband of my undersized suit. I don't think either of them moved from that chair the entire time.

"Mom?"

"Yes, Atlas?" Her voice quivered. It would do that off and on for many days to come.

"Is it ok if I go up to my room?"

She nodded and squeezed Hannah, nuzzling her chin into the side of my little sister's neck.

I stood to go upstairs just as Dad walked in the room. He stopped a couple steps inside the archway, just in front of his worn recliner. His tie was loosened and his top shirt button was undone, but he was otherwise immaculate. He held a forest green paper plate loaded with some scraps of ham and a blob of marshmallow jello funk.

"Did anyone figure out who that weird guy with the bizarre speech was?" Dad asked.

"Meemaw thinks he's the guy down the street," Mom replied, "the one who's never talked to anybody."

Dr. Crankenstein, I thought.

That was what we called him. He'd moved into the city about the same time as Aamilah's family, which caused quite a stir in Pinesburg. An immigrant family and an eccentric recluse arriving at the same time – it was almost too much for the old redneck gossips to handle. He looked like a scientist, a mad scientist, which is how we ended up calling him Dr. Crankenstein.

"I b-b-b-bet she's r-r-r-right," I said as I walked past

Dad, and started up the stairs.

"I'll ask her later. She's in the kitchen making sense of the leftovers," Dad replied. "I'm going to go out to the garage and get some work done."

"How can you work right now?" Mom asked. Her tears intensified at the end of the sentence so the word right now came out sounding like *wy ow*.

"I just can." Dad replied, unflinching. "Everyone grieves differently, Meredith."

"Atlas?" Dad turned to me.

"Yes?" I replied as I lifted my too-tight loafer onto the next step.

"Where are you going? You should probably stay with your mother."

I turned and looked down at him. I couldn't wait to get to my room. To get away. To be alone.

"I'm going up to my room," I replied, "Mom says it's ok."

"Are you sure, Meredith?" Dad asked Mom without looking at her.

"Yes. Yes." I heard her muffled voice reply through Hannah's hair.

"Ok. But don't stay there all night. It's good to get outside every once in a while, instead of playing make-believe. You're twelve years old, after all."

I nodded and kept climbing the stairs.

"We all grieve differently, Dad." I whispered as I

turned down the hallway and entered my room.

CHAPTER 5

As I walked into my room, I tripped over a box of old toys. I didn't even try to stop myself. I tumbled to the floor and just barely got my hands down before smacking my face on the cold wood floor. The box had been sitting near the doorway since I dug it out from the back of the closet the night Charlie died. Nothing was more fun than playing on the floor with our toy soldiers. He was always General Patton. I was usually General Grant, from the Civil War. It didn't fit history, but it fit us.

My head hurt, and it wasn't from the fall. I was filled with that drained dull ache that comes whenever you go too long without good sleep.

I lay on my side, closed my eyes and did nothing

but breathe. After a few minutes, I scanned the room. Everything was blurry. Slowly, my focus returned, and I noticed the science folder I'd been missing for a month. It was in the corner under the bunk bed, peeking out from under my pajama pants. Near the pants, a couple pieces of hard green candy coated with gray dust stared back at me like square ominous eyes.

I rolled over, sat up, and folded my legs under me – "criss-cross applesauce" – Hannah would say. I rummaged through the box and my daydreaming powers instantly transported me to another night, a much better night than any of the past week.

"I get the tanks," I said as I grabbed three camouflage painted metal rectangles. The rubber track wheel was torn off two of them, but they still had plenty of firepower.

"No, you don't," Charlie replied, "Ulysses Grant didn't have tanks."

"So?" I clutched them tighter and moved toward the space under the desk. I shoved the rolling chair out of my way and crawled underneath. I burrowed deeply into the spot.

"Home base," I said.

"Whatever," Charlie replied, "General Grant wouldn't even know what to do with the tanks. He wouldn't have any soldiers who could drive them. Or shoot them."

Charlie was always realistic. He didn't have much of an imagination, but he still tried to play along. I think he liked my daydreams. At the very least, he never belittled me. Which, in my pyramid of personal relationships, made him the capstone, just above Wyatt.

"Yeah, but he's on the fifty dollar bill," I retorted.

"Ha! What's that got to do with driving a tank? What's that got to do with winning a war?" He held his biggest soldier up. It had a detachable pith helmet and a bullwhip that was borrowed from some wilderness adventure toy set we got three or four Christmases earlier.

"This guy," Charlie announced, "General Patton. Now, he knew what to do with a tank!"

"Yeah but he didn't get his picture on any money," I said.

I squished further under the desk and elbowed the power strip to make room for my backside. As I pushed against the power strip, the bundle of brown wires jutting out from it nudged the metal trash bin off balance. As it collided with the floor, scraps of tissue and wadded up paper spilled out.

I dropped the tanks and slid out from my home base. As I stood up, I glanced back at the cardboard box that held our toys. Charlie wasn't holding General Patton. Charlie wasn't there at all. I studied the garbage on the floor through my suddenly teary eyes.

A folded yellow strip of paper caught my eye. It floated like an airplane emergency raft in the middle of a stormy ocean of white and brown scraps.

That looks like paper from Charlie's notepad.

I reached down and slid it against the wood floor as I snatched it. Like a match striking the side of a box, the unfolding of the note set my heart ablaze. Teardrops fell freely, splashing my arms and socks as I gulped and gurgled my way through the poorly spelled words. Charlie was good at sports, not English.

Dear Atlas,

I ben itching to tell you some things lately. I know you got a lot of dreams. They are cool. I wished I was smart like you. I don't always appreskiate what you like. I don't always ~~understand~~ ~~figure out~~ ~~know how to say~~

Coach Jefferson said something last week and I can't hardly get it out my brains. He said we got to never change what we was made to be, no matter what other people think. I see you all the time playing alone, lost in day dreaming and I know you feel kinda diffrent. I think you should be yourself. Keep dreaming, because nobody will ever

That was all there was. It ended, like Charlie's life, woefully incomplete. I read it through and through, and through again. Big brothers are the most curious mixture of hero, playmate, tyrant, conspirator, deserter, and friend. But in the end, they are family. And the good ones always remember this. Charlie was a good one. Charlie *is* a good one.

CHAPTER 6

The next two weeks slid by slower than the daily caravan of dump trucks rumbling up from the quarry with exhaust spewing plumes of black smoke. Every jarring bump on the poorly maintained road sent rocks spraying in all directions. Like those trucks, every conversation about Charlie spewed emotions like spent carbon fumes. Every comment about Charlie's life felt like loose gravel bouncing around the house. Each one hit my heart harder than the last.

School was school. The fog of grief shrouded and clouded my head. The days passed in a déjà vu like sequence of lonely lunches with Wyatt and staring at the back of Aamilah's head.

I hardly saw Dad. I guess he was working. Mom stayed on the couch most every day, crying and flipping through our family picture albums.

On back-to-back Sundays, Meemaw got all of us, except Dad, to church. She used every opportunity to get us in the Lord's house, and Charlie's death was no exception.

The second Sunday after Charlie's funeral, we were seated halfway back, in Meemaw's usual pew. Hannah grabbed a mini pencil and some offering envelopes and drew pictures of animals. I tried not to squirm.

Brother Westler made a point of welcoming us to the service. As he stood ten feet tall on the elevated stage, behind the giant mahogany plank podium, he peered down at us over his reading glasses.

"A special welcome to the Forman family. We continue to mourn with those who mourn," he announced. A few dozen silver haired heads bobbed in response.

"And," he continued, in a transition as ill-fitting as his burgundy polyester suit, "as the apostle Paul said, 'we rejoice with those who rejoice.' Today is baby dedication Sunday, and we have the Miller family here to commit their little one to the Lord."

The rest of the day got no better, and by the time I woke after two snooze buttons on Monday morning, I was actually looking forward to school.

"What do you want for breakfast?" Mom asked as I stumbled into the kitchen.

"Whatever," I mumbled while wedging myself onto the cushioned bench seat between the table and the bay window.

"Well, we've got hash browns and sausage that Meemaw made, and I think there's some cereal in the pantry. Is Hannah getting dressed for school?"

"I don't know. I guess I'll have the hash browns," I replied.

Mom scooped a pile of brown and white shredded potatoes out of the skillet and dumped it on a disposable plastic plate. She pitched two meat circles on top and slid the plate under my nose.

"Orange juice is on the counter if you want some; I'm going up to wake your sister."

I stared at the white globs of congealed grease embedded in the sausage. I poked at the equally grease drenched hash browns and forced down a few bites. After gulping some orange juice from the container, I left it on the counter and bounded up the stairs to get my tennis shoes for P.E.

"What's wrong honey?" I heard mom ask Hannah in the room across the hall.

I paused at the top of the stairs to eavesdrop.

"My tummy hurts," Hannah whimpered.

"My goodness, you're warm. It's ok baby, you can stay home today. Atlas?"

"Yes mom?" I answered as I released my grip on the

41

top knob of the wobbly banister.

"Come here."

I walked into Hannah's room. The pink and white explosion of paint on her walls made me feel like I was walking into a cotton candy factory. Too bad it didn't smell like one.

"It stinks! What's that smell?" I asked, pinching my nose.

"Don't be rude, Atlas. Your little sister isn't feeling well. I'm going to take her to see Doctor Wilson so you'll need to catch the bus." She looked at her watch. "Hurry up, it'll be at the end of the street in five minutes."

"Isn't Doctor Wilson retired? If not, he should be. He's so old. You sure you want her going to see him?" I asked, still pinching my nose.

"He's a good doctor, Atlas. If you can't say anything nice…"

"Yeah, I know. Say something untrue." I finished her statement with one of Marty's classic lines.

"No. That's not it, Atlas Michael Forman." Mom's face glowed and her eyes glinted like ice blue sapphires under jewelry store lighting. She stood up but kept one hand gently rubbing Hannah's midsection.

"I don't need your smart mouth right now. You know your father doesn't want us to go to the other doctor," she whispered as she continued, "you know, the new doctor."

"Oh, I know the new doctor, Mom. He's all the old

rednecks that run this town can talk about."

"Mind your tongue, Atlas. Sometimes you are too smart for your own good," she shook her head. "just get out of here! Go on, get to school." She pointed toward the front of the house.

"Yes Mom," I replied.

I went into my room and shoved my untouched homework into my backpack and scanned the room to check if I'd forgotten anything. My bed was unmade, which would get me another scolding from Mom. I couldn't miss the bus, though. That would be worse.

As I turned to go, a folded piece of yellow paper on my desk caught my eye. *Charlie's note.*

I grabbed it and tucked it in the outside pocket of my backpack, and sprinted down the steps.

"Three minutes, Atlas!" Mom shouted.

I grabbed the front doorknob and yanked.

"Atlas!"

It was Dad this time, calling from upstairs.

"I have to catch the bus!" I replied without turning.

"Did you make your bed?"

"I'll get it later!" I yelled, now in the middle of the front porch. I hurdled the broken concrete on the sidewalk and was nearly at full speed when Dad's voice carried into the street through the open hall window.

"That boy. I swear he lives in another world!"

Down the street, my school's rusty yellow and black

road schooner rolled up to the corner pick-up spot. I waved my arms over my head and shouted, "Wait!"

CHAPTER 7

I was breathing heavy as I climbed the sticky rubber steps into that green vinyl-seat-filled hormone soup known as Pinesburg Middle School bus #4. Moving down the rows, no one offered me a spot. The single-seaters slid toward the aisle, silently declaring no vacancy. Even Macy "Acne-Facy" Huddleston pushed her bookbag onto the edge of her bench.

I finally reached an open seat just a few rows from the back. Few dared enter the very back, the domain of Big Harold, school bully. He'd pursued and punished many a child for as long as I could remember. Dread drifted through the air like the smell of Meemaw's Lucky Strikes.

Ms. Turpentine had barely shifted the sixty-seat jalopy

into second gear when I heard his oafish voice taunting me from the back of the bus.

"Atlas the dreamer, Atlas the freak, Atlas ain't got no hope; anyway, anyday, every single week!"

I lowered my head and slowly unzipped the outside pocket of my backpack. Big Harold was as relentless as he was ignorant. He was either a early bloomer or a late starter, because he was bigger than any seventh grader I'd ever seen. Easily six feet tall and three lockers wide with a mop of curly brown hair and an ever-present scowl that caused his eyes to disappear behind dark lashes and puffy cheeks, some of the kids avoided his ire. Not me.

"Leave him alone. You know his brother just died," a dreamy delicate voice called out from a few rows ahead of me.

I lurched up and looked forward. Aamilah was turned around, facing me. Embarrassment sizzled across my face in a full-scale blush, so I looked back down at my backpack.

"Mind your own beeswax!" Harold yelled. "Go on back to Hajibaji on your magic carpet!"

"Atlas," he continued, "you gonna let a girl protect you?"

I glanced across the aisle. No help there, just a couple of squealy girls completely absorbed in the dush-dush-dush of the electronic beat blaring through their earbuds.

"You need to watch your mouth, Big – er Fat – Harold!" Aamilah shouted, not backing down.

46

"Aamilah, you need to sit down," Ms. Turpentine called out over her shoulder. The bus jolted and twenty floating heads in front of me simultaneously bobbed as we hit a road crater.

"Yes ma'am." Aamilah replied and lowered herself onto her seat.

Maybe everyone will calm down now. Maybe Harold will leave me alone if I just ignore him.

I pulled Charlie's note out, unfolded it, and smoothed it flat against my leg.

"Hey Atlas, how about you tell me your latest daydream? Oh, that's right, you can't talk with-with-with-without st-st-st-stut-stut-stuttering!"

Wishful thinking.

The bus slowed down to pick up the next batch of drowsy compulsory education victims. As it stopped, a foot jammed me forward through the back of my seat.

"Whatcha got there, Atlas?" Big Harold thundered.

I didn't reply.

He kicked me again. "I said, what you got there, Atlas? Is it a love note from your little red-dot lover? Can she even write English?"

"At l-l-l-least sh-sh-sh-she can r-r-read!" I shouted back.

The bus surged forward as it moved into a higher gear, flipping me back in my seat. As it did, the beefy paw of Big Harold seized the note from my hand.

I jumped to my feet.

"Give th-th-th-that b-b-back!" I shouted.

Harold held it overhead and danced in his seat. His thumping feet pounded the floor as I lunged across the bench, trying to grab my note. His freckle-splattered cheeks flapped as he mocked me. His unkempt bushy brown mane hung into his eyes. He looked like a sheepdog, but he acted like a rat terrier.

"Ooh, I got your attention now, huh loverboy? I hope you don't kiss like you t-t-t-talk! Aamilah's lips would be chapped!" He roared with laughter and waved the note high above me.

I jumped up onto the seat to even our height and reached for the note. Harold flattened me with his forearm, driving his beefy elbow into my chest. I tumbled backward and banged my head on the back of the seat in front of mine.

I was undeterred but probably would have fought less if it was a note from Aamilah. While clawing back up into my seat, I glanced her way.

Just like at Charlie's funeral, her misty dark eyes stared straight into my heart. She nodded as if to say, "keep going, fight back."

This time, I wouldn't back down. This was the only meaningful thing I had from my big brother. My only brother. My dead brother.

"You are n-n-nothing b-b-b-but a b-b-big f-f-faggot!"

I shouted and swung my fist wildly. Like a swarm of angry bees buzzing around an oak tree, I flailed and thrashed against him. And like a bee losing its stinger, I was going to hurt him even if it killed me. So consumed was I with retrieving my note, I failed to notice the hush that fell over the bus when that dreadful word flew from my lips.

The bus stopped as I leaped toward Big Harold. As our bodies collided, he stepped backward and my momentum flung us both into the bench beside him, onto a couple more squealy girls, who, now flattened against the window by Harold's haunches, squealed.

I scarcely noticed. My eyes were fixed on that yellow slip of paper and I scratched his fat arms and neck in desperation while scaling his ogre frame. The girls continued squealing.

"Get off me!" Big Harold shouted, revealing less strength than I expected as he swung his fists wildly at me. Most of the blows glanced off me. I think one of the squealy girls actually got the worst of it.

I took several shots to the chest and face. But before Big Harold could pull himself up and off the suffocating girls, I snatched the note.

"Got it!" I shouted in victory and turned to run to my seat.

I had hoped to savor the moment. Never once had any student challenged Big Harold with success. Alas, no sooner had I wrestled the note away when I was greeted by an equally ogre-ish adversary.

Ms. Turpentine grabbed my neck and tossed me into the seat. Unlike Harold's illusory size-strength correlation, she was full of raw power. Her thick arms and vice-like fingers bore witness to a life of labor as they bore down on my tender skin. The soles of my shoes kicked my own butt as the force of her shove bent me nearly in half. My face squished against the thick vinyl seat as she pushed me.

"SIT DOWN!" She shouted.

It took a lot to get her out of the driver's seat. Obviously, we'd done it. Or, I'd done it. As her fourth chin vibrated with rage, she stormed around my seat, shouting about juvenile delinquents, and "kids these days". Strong, yes. Original, no.

As she yelled, "I can't believe you, Atlas," I rolled over and sat up. I stared at the moles clustered like a solar system across her upper chest. They were arranged in an elliptical pattern, and the biggest one, like Jupiter, had several freckle moons.

It would be cool to go to the moon.

In a blink, I was there and exiting the lunar module hatch. A weird blur of lights flickered from the stars. Protocol demanded that I clarify the coordinates with headquarters during the descent to the lunar surface.

"Fifteen degrees northwest, Caspian crater descent zone. Surface temperature one hundred seventeen degrees Celsius."

"The temperature is going to be hotter than that for you!" Ms. Turpentine's booming admonition shattered my brief daydream.

"It's going to be real hot when you get to Principal Wilkins office. Now, sit there and don't move until we get to the school."

She swung her bulging body around and faced Big Harold.

"And you, Mr. Instigator, come up front. You're riding with me the rest of the way."

As the two biggest humans on the bus made their way past me, I watched them go with a measure of regret for what loomed ahead but held my note tightly, pleased with my unexpected strength. I bit my lip firmly, fearful of my soon-coming visit to Principal Wilkins' office.

Agony grew within me as my mind weighed the implications of the impending visit, and the likely additional consequences of punishment at home. My heart sank. I looked down at the now crumpled yellow paper. I had my note. Whatever was going to happen next, the fight was worth it.

As the wide loads ambled past the benches, Aamilah's face came into view like the sun on the backside of an eclipse. Her eyes smiled. Her smile smiled.

It was enough to make me smile.

CHAPTER 8

Principal Wilkins waiting room was dank. Dank is one of those words that sounds like its meaning. I can't remember what those words are called. The receptionist's cold metal desk was just far enough away to avoid my swinging feet, but close enough to make our shared silence, only interrupted by the occasional shrill ring of the telephone, as awkward as possible.

I squirmed in the plastic folding chair, which was perfectly positioned in the door side window giving all passing students a view of the latest rule-breaker.

Many were the days I'd passed through that hall before pausing briefly to stare at the latest student offender. If our eyes met, I'd nod in solidarity, supportive of their plea of innocence. If not, I'd conjure up an imagined wickedness perpetrated by the hoodlum seated in this selfsame plastic chair.

"Atlas." A female voice called from the far side of the room.

My expectation had been to hear the somber tone of Principal Wilkins. I looked up in surprise as she continued.

"Come 'ere young mon." Before I saw who was speaking, I knew. Ms. Pendleton's soft Carribean accent was instantly recognizable. Especially in Pinesburg, Kentucky.

Ms. Pendleton was the school counselor. She was tall and lean and had come to our community as a student teacher after swimming as a scholarship athlete for the University. Twelve years later, she was still single but had adopted two children. By far, she was the most exotic resident of Pinesburg.

Her arms were folded across her chest, and her V-shaped face was tilted to one side. She tried to scare me with her forced grimace, but the smile in her eyes reminded me she was my guardian angel, come straight from the heavens to rescue me from the devastating sentence sure to be handed down from Principal Wilkins.

I exhaled in relief as we entered her office.

She closed the door and walked behind the desk. As she sat down, she motioned for me to do the same.

I plopped onto one of the bright blue beanbags that Miss Pendleton used as visitors' chairs. The scrunching sound of thousands of tiny plastic beads under my body echoed through her small space.

"What a man child, evryting cool?" She asked with a grin.

"Evryting is ari," I answered in my best island accent.

"I wouldn't go that far, if I were you." She quickly dropped the island lingo and used her well-honed American accent as she sat at her maple desk. A double strand of pearls practically glowed against her dark skin. Her perfectly polished nails formed a shimmering row of rolling red hilltops as she folded her hands and leaned forward. The neatly stacked notebooks between us were the only obstruction on her otherwise pristine work surface.

"What happened on the bus today, Atlas?"

"B-b-big H-ha-harold," I began.

"Relax. Remember your breathing. Center yourself. You are safe here." She smiled and nodded as I gulped.

I closed my eyes. I could still see her smile. Ms. Pendleton - my confidant, my friend. My *savior.* I breathed slowly and began to speak. Without stuttering.

"I found a note from Charlie. It was a letter to me that he never finished. It is very special. When B-B-Big Har-harold," I paused and opened my eyes.

Relax. Just relax.

"When he took it," I continued, looking straight at Ms. Pendleton's kind eyes, "I sn-sn-snapped. I had to get it back."

She nodded and unfolded her hands.

My hands nervously crinkled the beanbag alongside my legs.

"Is that all?" She asked.

"I think so."

"Are you sure there's nothing else you want to talk about. Maybe something you said?"

I looked at the floor. The amoeba swirls on the throw rug were a confusing mix of orange, white, and pale yellow. Ms. Pendleton certainly liked things bright, especially her students. The second day of the year, she called me into her office to tell me she had reviewed my file and that I had one of the highest IQ test scores in school history. I told her it didn't matter how great my mind was, if I couldn't speak it.

Now, I had spoken a taboo word on the bus and I knew it meant detention, and possibly probation.

"Well," I replied, looking back at her, "I said a bad word. I called him a f-f-f-fag-faggot."

"Do you typically say that word?" She asked.

"No." I had probably heard it a few dozen times on the bus or in PE class, but it was not in my regular rotation of always unspoken insults.

"Why do you think you said it?" She asked.

"I wanted to hurt him. Somehow. I didn't think I could ph-ph-physically hurt him."

She leaned back in her chair. "Atlas, if I tell you something, can you promise to keep it just between us?"

"Yes ma'am."

"I've been called words like that before, Atlas. And it hurts."

I nodded and looked down.

"I can't imagine anyone c-c-c-alling someone as nice and pr-pr-pr-pretty as you a bad name, Miss Pendleton." I said.

"I don't expect you to understand. But, mostly I got called names because of my appearance. The boys who taunted me couldn't understand why, as they said, a pretty girl like me wasn't interested in dating them."

"Do me a favor, Atlas?" She stood to her feet.

"Yes ma'am?"

"Don't use that word ever again."

"Yes ma'am," I answered.

"Of course, Atlas, there are still consequences for your words. And your behavior." She pulled a manila envelope from the bookshelf behind her.

"Principal Wilkins wanted to suspend you for two days. I intervened. Of course, after you see the consequence, you might wish for suspension. Stand up. Come over here." She beckoned for me to walk over to the small filing cabinet against the far wall.

I followed the edge of the desk and turned to join her under an arrangement of rectangular certificates neatly hung on the brown wallpaper covered wall.

"This," she said, opening a manila folder and pulling

out several pieces of paper, "is your punishment."

CHAPTER 9

"She's making you enter the School District Spelling Bee? That's only a month away. Holy cow," Wyatt whistled.

"That's what I said," I replied.

We stared straight ahead as the bus bounced us into each other. What I thought was going to be Ms. Pendleton's heavenly rescue was really a toss into the worst possible hell.

"Well, Atlas, you are one of the danged smartest kids I know," Wyatt replied. His eyes scrunched almost closed as the turning bus brought sunlight pouring in our window.

"Whose side are you on?" I said as I punched him in the leg. "B-b-be-be-besi-si-si-sides. I can't d-d-d-do it. I can barely sp-speak without st-st-stut-stuttering when I'm with you. Mu-mu-much less on stage!"

Wyatt looked at me. I returned his stare.

"That hurt," he said, rubbing his thigh.

"Sorry," I replied.

"You know I ain't smart like you, Atlas, but I got horse sense. I reckon you can do it. You know how to spell all those ginormous words. It's just going to take practice. I'll lend you a hand." He smiled and tugged on his ever-present baseball cap.

His close-cropped blonde hair, just visible around the edge of his hat, reminded me of Wyatt's throwback ways. In a world that honors individualism, Wyatt was refreshingly anachronistic. It's like he stepped out of an old black and white TV show, where everyone said "yes ma'am" and men shaved every morning and wore a suit everyday.

I returned his smile. "Thanks for being such a goo-goo-good fr-fr-friend," I whispered. "At least I still got this." I held up a wrinkled piece of yellow paper.

"What's that?" Wyatt asked.

I unfolded it. "This is the last thing I have from Charlie. It's a letter I found that he started writing to me some time before he wa-wa-was k-k-ki-ki-killed."

"Oh man," Wyatt whispered. "That's what Big Harold tried to take from you? I can see why you called him a fa, fa…you know, that word."

"Well, I'm paying the price now. Spelling B-B-Bee for my pun-pun-punishment. L-L-Listen to me. I can b-b-barely talk to-to-to you."

"You can do it, Atlas. I know you can." Wyatt smiled and tossed his arm around my shoulder. "You're the smartest kid in school. And after seeing you fight Big Harold, I'd say one of the bravest."

"Thanks."

"And you know what else?" Wyatt asked.

"What?"

"You inspired me. Yes sir, I'm 'bout to do some damage to Big Harold myself."

"What do you mean?" I asked, leaning back in my seat.

"Remember the awesome rock I found a month or so ago? In our hideout?"

"Yes, that rock was very cool," I replied.

"Yeah, well, I think Big Harold stole it from me," Wyatt's eyes squinted as he glared out the window.

"Why do you think he stole it?" I asked.

"Who else would? Plus, a couple weeks ago, he was near my locker when I came walking out of the bathroom. He took off running. You don't think that's strange? For Big Harold to run away?"

"I guess so," I replied. I was not interested in another fight with Big Harold, even if he stole Wyatt's special rock.

"Anyway," Wyatt said, "since you stood up to him, I thought I'd make it so he'd have trouble standing up at all."

"Ain't this your stop, boys?" Ms. Turpentine called from the front of the bus.

I folded the note and pushed it into my pocket.

"Let's go," I said, "But don't bother with Big Harold."

"It's too late," Wyatt whispered.

We grabbed our backpacks from beneath our feet. I got about three steps when I caught Ms. Turpentine's glare in the wide rearview mirror atop the inside of the windshield. I politely nodded as I approached her seat, which was virtually swallowed by the extra layers of body that hung from her hips and thighs.

"I'm s-s-s-orry about th-th-this morning," I said.

She sniffed and adjusted her transition-lensed spectacles. I could barely see her eyes through the frosted glass. Her oily ponytail swung as she shook her head in a disappointed "no".

Wyatt pushed against me through my backpack.

"Wait for me, fellas," Big Harold called from somewhere behind Wyatt.

I froze. Big Harold had a different stop from ours.

No sooner had he spoken than the entire bus shook. I glanced back to see Harold's massive body sprawled in the aisle of the bus, face down.

"Who tied my shoes together?!" He shouted as he squirmed to get up.

"It's a mystery," Wyatt said as he laughed.

"It was probably you, Atlas Forman. I'm gonna kill you!" Big Harold yelled. He rolled over and yanked his shoes off. He stood up in his socks, holding his shoes in his hand.

I looked at Ms. Turpentine for help. She shrugged her shoulders and held her palms up. Then she waved her fat mitts toward the door, shooing me off the bus. She didn't care what happened to me. Harold could beat the stuffin' out of me, as long as it wasn't on her bus.

I hustled out of the bus, with Wyatt close behind. The thundering hooves of Big Harold were closing in.

"Old Fat Harold, ain't you ashamed. You so fat, you can't play no games," Wyatt said.

"You got a problem, skinny boy?" Big Harold's shadow loomed over us as he descended the final steps of the bus.

"No problem we can't handle. You're a loser," Wyatt replied. He was not backing down. But I sure was. Without the motivation of getting my note, I was not interested in a fight.

I stepped down onto the cracked asphalt, noticing the faded yellow line painted in the center of the road. It used to shine like the sun, now it flickered like the end of a shooting star.

Time to shine. Time to fly.

A cluster of blinking lights suddenly surrounded me, urging me to run. They hovered and circled my body, pulsing me forward. I blasted off, tearing down the road. I was a human shooting star, a rocket ship. I streaked through the street, blinded to the sight of anything but the blinking lights.

They propelled me onto the sidewalk. I raced by house after house, oblivious to anything but my urge to escape contact with Big Harold. As I ran, the blinking lights morphed into miniature runners, bouncing along beside and behind me.

"Atlas, Atlas!" I heard them shout.

A group of them suddenly appeared along the sidewalk, like fans at a sporting event. Their blurred outlines appeared like a computer-generated crowd scene from an old video game.

"Atlas, Atlas!" The chant of the crowd increased as I approached the finish line – my front yard. The lights disappeared but the voices kept cheering.

"Atlas, Atlas!"

The miniature runners blurred into the air and I was once again alone. Yet, I could hear my name still being called.

"Atlas!"

It was Wyatt.

I decelerated as I crossed the sidewalk into my front yard. I dug my heels into the grass and slid to a halt and turned my head.

Wyatt looked like he was doing more wrestling than running. His backpack was swinging from side to side, barely clinging to the edge of his shoulder. He was dragging my backpack in his left hand and pinned his baseball cap to his head with his right hand. Sweat rained down his red cheeks.

"Atlas!" He shouted. "You try'na get me killed?"

I looked beyond Wyatt's fuming countenance. Big Harold was several front yards behind, bent over and heaving like he had been underwater longer than his lungs would allow. He shuddered as he gasped for air.

"I'm sorry, Wyatt. I forgot all about my backpack," I apologized. Wyatt slowed as he approached the corner of my front yard.

"You sure did. You took off like a trash-raiding coon caught in headlights. I didn't know you could run that fast!"

"I was carried by the lights," I said.

"What lights?" Wyatt asked.

"Never mind," I replied, "I was pretty fast, huh?"

"Yes. You were. Never seen that before."

"Thanks Wyatt. You always have my back." I chuckled. "And my backpack."

Wyatt flung my backpack at me. I caught it, and staggered, taking several steps back.

"It's not funny," Wyatt replied. "Why'd you run? You knew Big Harold was breathing down my neck."

"You started the fight with him, remember?" I asked.

"Yeah, so? I thought we were in this together."

"Sorry."

"I just wish I could understand your imagination. It's going to get us – or maybe just me – killed one of these days." Wyatt shook his head.

"It's my fault," I replied. "Look, we're ok now. What do you say? Is everything cool?" I raised my hand to give Wyatt a high five, hoping he'd calm down.

He reluctantly raised his hand. I smacked Wyatt's hand and bent down to grab my backpack. As I did, I looked down the sidewalk at our enemy.

Big Harold was standing upright now, half a block away, shaking his fist in the air. He reached to the ground and scooped up a chunk of rock. I watched him wind up and fling it; it flew straight as an arrow toward my unsuspecting friend.

"Wyatt! Watch out!" I shouted and lunged toward him.

I pushed Wyatt, shoving him to the soft cool grass. As I did, my own body stood completely exposed to the impending missile. My hands shot up to protect my face just in time. The rock smacked me in the forearm and ricocheted into my chin. I tumbled to the ground, tripped over Wyatt, and lay sprawled on the grass beside him.

"You ok?" He asked.

I looked at the clouds gathering overhead. The earth felt like it was spinning. I took a couple deep breaths.

"I think so. Gosh, I hate that fat punk," I whispered.

"What happened, Atlas?" Mom's voice intruded.

She was standing on the porch with a gingham dishtowel in her hand. She looked down the street, then back at us.

"Nothing, Mom," I replied.

"Don't lie to me, Atlas. Why is your arm dripping blood?"

I looked down at my right arm. A jagged ribbon of red snaked along its side. Small beads of crimson swelled until their weight caused them to drop to the ground.

"Oh, shoot. Look at th-tha-tha-that," I muttered.

"Who is that boy down the street?"

"Fat – er, Big Harold."

"Hmmm. He's not usually around here, is he?" She paused and stared down the street once more, then waved us into the house. "Come on, let's get you cleaned up."

CHAPTER 10

After patching up my arm, Mom gave us a snack to take up to my room. As we carried our plates of grilled cheese and apple slices, Wyatt noticed a stack of anti drunk driving propaganda on the hall table.

"Where'd that come from?" He asked as he turned to head up the stairs.

I followed close behind, although I had to pause to yank up my jeans. Both pockets were laden with juice pouches and I had already waddled the last couple steps.

"Mom," I answered, "She's getting pretty involved with a local group of parents in stopping drunk driving." I stopped and stared at the brochures. A bright red circle with a diagonal line overlaid a black and white sketch of beer cans and car keys.

"The prosecution wants to charge the guy with second degree m-m-m-murder instead of man-man-man-manslaughter," I said halfway up the steps. "I heard Dad talking about it yesterday. He's b-b-bud-bud-buddies with all the other attorneys, so he gets the inside scoop."

"Man, I'm so sorry, Atlas," Wyatt said. We reached the top of the stairs and walked to my room's threshold.

"Yeah," I said. I couldn't say anything else. The inside of my throat turned hot and my eyes started to water.

I followed Wyatt into my room. He sat on the edge of my bed and stretched his legs out. I pulled out our juice and tossed a pouch to him, then sat down at my desk and swiveled in my chair.

I bit into the gooey grilled cheese and instantly waved air into my open mouth.

"Hot. Hot," I gaped.

Wyatt laughed. He opened his mouth and bugged his eyes out and flapped his hands, aping me.

"Thanks, buddy," I said. The cheese atop my tongue felt like lava. I quickly plunged the plastic straw into my juice box, shooting a sweet tropical spray onto my arm and chest. I sucked the pina colada flavored beverage and swished it in my mouth, vainly trying to quench the burning cheese on my tender tongue.

"Man, you're having a bad day," Wyatt said as he popped an apple slice into his mouth. He started to list the horrors of my last twelve hours.

"Fight with Big Harold, Meeting with Miss Pendleton, Spelling Bee, Hit by a rock…"

"Enough aweady," I cut him off. "I'd be fine with-with-without B-Big Harold." My tongue felt swollen and I sounded like I had the world's worst sinus infection.

"Gwait. Just gwait."

"We still have five and a half years to live with that guy, at least. It's going to be forever before we finish high school. We need to do something to get him off our backs. I know he stole my rock. And he hit you with one. We need to get revenge," Wyatt said.

"Are you theriouth?" I asked. My burnt tongue lisp was getting worse by the second.

"Yes. Eat your apple. Maybe that will help your tongue," Wyatt suggested. He stood up and transferred his plate from his lap to my bed.

"Now, let's figure out a plan to get back at Big Harold. He doesn't have any friends, so the two of us should be able to do something that puts him in his place. We're smart enough. At least you are."

"But, I'm aweady in twouble," I replied.

"We have to," Wyatt insisted. "We have to stand up to him or he'll just push us around all through high school. I'm not try'na do anything too dangerous, just enough to spook him. Enough to make him think twice about messing with us." Wyatt turned to his plate and took a big bite of his now cool-enough grilled cheese.

"Ok," I said. "But what?"

"Something that'll embarrass him right good. Nothing that'll get us in real trouble, you know, but enough to put him in his place." Wyatt turned back to me and placed his hands on his hips. He was intent on revenge and his mind was relishing the possibilities.

"Pwoblem is, we aren't good at making twouble," I said.

Wyatt rubbed his chin and walked to the corner of my room. He stared up at a poster Dad had hung on the wall a few years before.

"Yes, yes. That'll do the trick," Wyatt whispered as he studied the image of a soot-covered miner climbing out of a hole, headlamp glowing. Those Who Work Hard Shine Bright was printed in yellow block letters against the black background.

"I've got it!" Wyatt smacked his hands together and turned to face me. "Stand up, Atlas." He waved me back. "No, no, sit down. This is a doozy. Gonna fix Big Harold up right good. Ha!" He laughed.

"What?! What is it?!" I asked.

"Ok. We're going to set up a trap. We need a large bucket. I can get one from my house. Then, I'll get a bunch of fish heads from my grandma's pig slop trough."

"What for?" I interjected.

"I'm going to chop 'em up real fine. Then, we'll put 'em

in the bucket with some water. We'll strap it up in a tree, with a rope coming down." He slid his hands toward the ground, like he was unbundling a coil of rope. "And I'll get him to chase me." Wyatt pointed at me.

"Why you p-p-p-pointing at me?" I asked.

"This is where you come in. I'll bring him by the tree, and you'll pull the rope, dumping it all on him." Wyatt stepped back, folded his arms and smiled. He winked at me. "How about that?"

"Umm. I don't know," I replied. "That doesn't seem like it would c-c-c-cause him to st-st-stop picking on us. Where do you plan on doing it? What tr-tr-tr-trees?" I asked.

"The ones backside of the gymnasium at school. That way everyone will see him," Wyatt answered.

"Everyone will see us, too. Including a t-t-t-teacher – or Principal Wilkins. Seems to me," I replied, "that it would be safer and s-s-sm-sm-smarter," I tapped the side of my head, "to do it where there aren't any witnesses. He's less likely to come after us if no-no-nobody sees."

"But, that's half the point," Wyatt said, "doing it where no one could see would be like throwing rocks at a ten-point buck. It might sting him a little, but you ain't getting no rack mounted in the house, and you ain't getting no meat neither," Wyatt said.

"I know, but," I stood up, "We're not h-h-h-hunting deer. We're getting back at the school b-b-b-bully. The most important thing to him is making sure everyone th-th-thinks he's the man. Making sure everyone is scared of him. If we show him up in f-f-f-front of everybody, he'll have no choice but to go after us."

Wyatt looked at me like Marty used to when Meemaw would try to get him to go to a volunteer work day at the church, painting the walls or fixing a leaky faucet, that kind of thing.

"Ain't my burden," he'd say, "I didn't break their faucet. Besides, I'd sooner go corn shucking with one-arm Freddie than I'd go paint a church."

Though he appeared in many of Marty's expressions and excuses, I never met one-arm Freddie. Wyatt had no such straw man, but he remained unconvinced. I needed both my arms and all my wits to convert him to my position on the matter.

"Look," I said, "If we do someth-th-th-th-thing at school, we'll end up getting punished there. One spelling bee is enough."

Wyatt's expression slowly morphed from consternation to resignation.

"Fine. I suppose. But I ain't happy that I won't be able to show off that big buck's rack. Never minding not having any jerky." Wyatt said.

"What?" I shook my head. "You make as much sense as Marty sometimes."

"Who?"

"Never mind," I answered.

"If we aren't doing it at school, then where?" Wyatt asked.

"How about the woods behind Dr. Crankenstein's place? How about the abandoned mine shaft?" I asked.

Wyatt nervously shifted his weight back and forth on his feet as he considered my proposal.

"Not our hideout. That's our place."

"I know," I replied. "That's our home turf. I'd never reveal it to anyone. I'm talking about the caved-in part of the t-t-t-tunnels, about two hundred yards be-be-beyond our spot. In the clearing near the fence line of Dr. Crankenstein's yard."

I anxiously looked at Wyatt. He stopped his fidgeting feet and crossed his arms, like it was settled.

"I like it," he nodded. "I can see him now, like some wild varmint, stuck in the ground. Then you dump the bucket of fish guts down the hole, and he'll be covered in slop. Ooh boy, he's gonna regret messing with us. He's gonna be fit to be tied." Wyatt slapped his thigh and tossed his head back. As he laughed, he looked like a coyote howling at the moon.

I sat grinning and eating, impressed with our – my – plan.

"I know the perfect time for it," Wyatt said.

"When's that?" I asked as I shoved my favorite strip of sandwich, the delicious crust, into my finally pain-free mouth.

"Tomorrow morning. At the bus stop. Like I said, let's strike while the egg is still in the nest."

"What? How are we going to do it tomorrow morning? Big Harold doesn't ev-ev-even go on our st-st-stop," I replied.

"He gonna be there all this week," Wyatt whispered.

"Why are you whispering?" I asked. "There's no one here."

"It just feels like I should. You know, like whenever people plot a sinister plan, they have to be real quiet. Never know when Johnnie Law might be listening." Wyatt knelt down on one knee.

"Johnnie Law? What are you t-t-t-talking about?" I was getting annoyed. It wasn't going to be easy to trap Big Harold. We certainly weren't going to make it easier by acting silly.

"Come on, Atlas. You're the king of daydreaming. Can't I just have a little fun? A little make-believe?" Wyatt teased.

"I guess. I'll pl-pl-play along. You were saying?"

"Cool. Now, I'll plan on getting to the bus stop early. Big Harold is staying with his uncle down the street because his dad just got put in jail. Heard him telling a bunch of juniors and seniors that they could come there this weekend for a party."

"His dad got put in jail?" I asked, "How do you know?"

"It was in the newspaper. He was part of a group of jewelry thieves. Probably explains why Big Harold stole my rock. I know it's got pieces of diamond in it!"

"You read the newspaper?" I asked.

"Yeah. Sometimes, why?"

"I never figured you for the reading type. Anyway, are you going to get the bucket of fish guts?"

"Yes," Wyatt snapped his fingers. "That's right. Right as applesauce after losing a bunch of teeth." He stood up. "I'm going to get the fish bucket made up. We might need to dig out around the hole. It's probably overgrown with weeds and stuff. Can you get a couple shovels and meet me in our spot in the woods in one hour?"

I held out my hand for a shake.

Wyatt gripped it firmly. Our deal was done. Our plan was set. With that, Wyatt walked out of my room. I remained alone, thinking about our scheme. It wasn't the most sophisticated or original method of revenge, but it would do the trick. Or, so we hoped.

CHAPTER 11

Twenty minutes later, I was in the garage, scaling a mountain of tightly packed cardboard boxes so I could reach the shovels mounted high above on the pegboard wall.

"Whatcha doin'?" A sweet faint voice drifted up from somewhere on the smooth concrete below.

I looked over my shoulder cautiously. I had a good grip and my feet were wedged in between the boxes and the metal rack holding Dad's collection of old Corvette parts, but I couldn't be too careful. One slip and I'd be buried under an avalanche of junk-filled corrugated boxes. My little sister peaked through the side doorway, her round face nearly as shiny as the golden doorknob she held as she leaned on the door.

"Hey Hannah," I answered. "I'm just getting a couple shovels. "What are you doing?"

"I'm following you."

"Why are you following me?" I asked.

"If I follow you, I can make sure you won't be dead like Charlie."

My heart flopped and my chin started to quiver.

Don't cry. Don't. Cry.

I plucked the shovels from the wall and pushed back from the stack of boxes like I was rappelling down a cliff, except I had no rope or harness. I dropped to the ground, managing to keep my feet under me. The shovels weren't as lucky. My grip slipped and they clanged against the hard surface.

I ignored my digging tools and turned to Hannah.

"Don't worry, Han. I'm not g-g-g-going to die."

"How do you know?" She asked. "Everyone dies, don't they?"

"Well." I had to think. There was no easy answer, no matter how long I stood there.

"Well what?" Hannah asked.

"Well," I said as I picked up a shovel and walked over to her. "S-S-See this shovel?"

"Yes," she answered, her moist eyes twinkling. She was an easy-going, carefree kid. It was hard to lose Charlie, but watching Hannah lose her innocence was, in some ways, even worse.

"Th-Th-Th-This sh-shovel," I continued, "was just hanging here. It's been in this garage since before I was born. It wasn't doing anything. Until I picked it up. Now, I'm going to put it to use. I'm kinda like that. I've been here since before you were born. And whenever you need me, you can find me. Like this sh-sh-shovel, I'll help you. And I won't break."

My analogy wasn't particularly strong. Then again, my knack for comfort isn't particularly well-developed.

Hannah's green eyes sparkled as she stepped next to me.

"You are strong like the shovel?" She asked.

"Yes," I replied.

"Well, I don't really need a shovel. I need a hug." She held up her chubby hands.

I dropped the shovel instantly and scooped her up in my arms. I pulled her close. The smell of peanut butter and jelly filled my nostrils.

"Did you have a peanut butter sandwich?" I asked.

Her little head nodded against my shoulder.

"I'll make you a deal, Han," I said. "Anytime you need a hug, you just clap your hands. Ok?"

"Ok," she whispered in my ear.

I put her back on the ground and turned to grab the shovels. The sound of her hands clapping startled me but made me smile. We embraced once more.

"I'll be back soon," I said as I picked up the shovels.

She latched onto my leg as I exited the garage, shovels over my shoulder.

"Just remember, Atlas. I will be here when you're done."

"I know Han, I know," I replied.

As I walked through the side yard, I heard a faint clapping sound. I turned and looked back. In the doorway of the garage stood Hannah, outstretched arms.

"I'll give you a hug as soon as I get home!" I yelled.

I turned to go and spotted Wyatt halfway down the street, sloshing a giant paint bucket as he walked.

"Wait up!" I shouted.

CHAPTER 12

Wyatt stopped near the front of Dr. Crankenstein's house, which was about seven houses down from mine, near the end of the street, beside the school bus stop. I hustled to catch up to him, shovels clanging against each other with every footfall.

"You got it?" I asked breathlessly.

"Yes." He lifted the bucket up as best he could to show me. "Thing's harder to move than a two-legged hog. But, it's ready."

"Smells like it." I waved my hand in front of my nose.

We stood there a second, near the corner of the driveway.

"Let's get moving," Wyatt said. "This place gives me

the creeps. You know, Epson said the other day he saw a couple stray dogs nosing around that garage," he said as he pointed to the strange hieroglyphic covered panel on the garage door, "and the next day they were dead."

"That's crazy," I replied. "But Epson's always m-m-m-making up st-st-stuff. Besides, you think Crankenstein would really kill d-d-dogs?"

"How should I know? It's not like anybody's ever talked to him. Come on. Let's git going." Wyatt started sloshing away. "The longer we are out on the street, the more chance Big Harold's gonna come after us."

"All right." I followed after Wyatt, but I didn't want to drop the issue of Crankenstein's alleged dog killing. As we reached the end of the street and turned left past the fire hydrant where Wyatt once busted out a couple teeth in an unfortunate broken bike speedometer accident, I resumed the conversation.

"I know everybody's got their theory on the man. We've only seen him a couple times in nearly a year, and each time he had on a white lab coat. I think he's a scientist, like a forensics guy. Whatever he's doing, I don't think it involves dog dissections. Plus, how do you explain that weird lettering on that one board of his garage door?"

"I think it's some cult symbols or maybe he worships Satan. That would explain the dead dogs, too," Wyatt replied, "I think he's up to no good. I mean, he's been here almost a year and he ain't never met nobody. Not one conversation. I don't care where you're from, he's nuttier than the bottom of a port-a-potty at the peanut festival."

"I'm not saying it was him or not, but the stuff he said at Charlie's funeral was kinda cool. L-L-L-Like he's from olden times."

"At Charlie's funeral?" Wyatt's eyes widened. "Oh yeah, now I remember. That's right!" Wyatt said. "I forgot about that. What do you think that was about?"

"I don't know –"

"I know. He's a psychic. He was givin' a prophecy about you. I remember he said something about an atlas. That's your name!" Wyatt said.

"Yes, it is," I replied.

"Hey," Wyatt said, looking at the sky. "We're going to run out of time. We need to get moving." He picked up the bucket and started walking toward the end of the road.

I followed him, shovels in hand. "At least your theory about Crankenstein isn't as st-st-stupid as some of the b-b-b-boys at school."

Last year, when Dr. Crankenstein first showed up in Pinesburg, a couple of boys said they'd seen him at the pharmacy buying all kinds of vials and liquids and powders. Some said he was a warlock, come to cast spells on us for letting Aamilah's dad come to be a doctor at our county hospital.

Big Harold was the worst of all. "Once you let one of them camel herders in, they'll soon have a whole village running around wearing bathrobes and chattering jibberish," he had said.

"But, I do wonder - how do you explain the weird letters on the garage door?" Wyatt asked.

"Exactly!" I exclaimed. "I don't have to explain them. *They* explain him."

We reached the end of the side street that marked the end of the residential development. After turning and walking the length of the last house's back yard, we entered the heavily treed area – a greenbelt is what the grown-ups called it – that separated our neighborhood from the next developed area a mile or so away. On the other side of that greenbelt was the cemetery. The same spot where the tuberculosis epidemic stopped spreading back in the 1800's.

"The letters are symbols," I said. "Maybe he's into ancient languages. That would explain his strange way of t-t-t-talking."

We wound through the trees on the well-worn trail that Wyatt and I had traveled many times before. I swatted at a cloud of gnats that hovered between us and the last turn in the trail before the back of Crankenstein's place. Before our hideout.

Wyatt plunked his bucket down and rubbed his arms.

"I need a break. Man, them fish pieces are heavy."

"No problem. Catch your breath." I dropped one shovel to the ground and leaned on the handle of the other.

Wyatt leaned against a tree trunk and said, "Just

remember, I'm the one who came up with his nickname."

"Crankenstein?" I asked. "It's a pretty lame name, you know?"

"So? You're Mr. English, not me. I'm just a good ol' country boy!"

"You got that right," I laughed, "and I wouldn't h-h-have it any other way.

"Good." Wyatt smiled and tugged on his baseball cap. He reached down for his bucket. "I'm ready when you are."

"Let's hurry and get this done. It would be fun to visit our cave. I haven't been in there since Charlie d-d-d-died."

"It's a deal," Wyatt replied. "Let's go."

CHAPTER 13

Clank. Clank.

Wyatt and I drove our shovels into the ground. We were breaking up the mounded soil and grass that surrounded the caved-in tunnel where hopefully, Big Harold would end up the next day. Wyatt wanted to widen the spot to make sure it was big enough to swallow Big Harold.

The whole tunnel wasn't more than eight feet deep and nearly as narrow as my petite mother's waist. Thirty minutes had passed, and we were halfway done expanding the opening when Wyatt's shovel repeatedly rang like an old church bell.

Clank. Clank.

"You're hitting something," I said.

He dropped the shovel and shook his hands. "No kidding! Man that stings." He slid to his knees and began scraping around the area.

"Big rock?" I asked and squatted down along the lip of the hole and peered over his bony shoulders.

"I don't think so," he answered. He clawed at the cool soil, ignoring centipedes and rolly-pollys that scampered away from his fingers.

"Really?" I stepped into the hole beside him and began to scrape at the dirt.

"See!" Wyatt exclaimed. "That ain't no rock!"

He leaned back and pointed at a long straight edge of metal glimmering in the sunlight that crept through the trees.

"What is that?" I whispered.

"Help me dig," Wyatt replied, furiously pawing at the dirt.

I grabbed my shovel with both hands and held it near the blade. The long handle wavered overhead as I used it like Meemaw hoeing her cucumber patch. Wyatt continued scratching around the object with his hands.

We kept working until we exposed a metal rectangle about two feet long. The corners were bracketed with stainless steel and the surface was a dark faded bronze with etchings all over it.

"It's some kind of c-c-case. Maybe it's f-f-f-full of

money," I said.

"Oh my gosh. Can you imagine?" Wyatt asked.

He lifted his baseball cap and tugged off his t-shirt.

"What are you doing?" I asked.

"I don't have a rag. This'll work," he replied. He began to wipe the surface clean of dirt with his wadded up shirt.

"Good idea," I said. I joined him.

Suddenly, two skinny shirtless boys were leaning over a narrow pit, swiping at the top of what we hoped was a briefcase full of money. We were beginning to see the etchings clearly when a shrieking sound jolted us up stiffer than the quills on an angry mama porcupine.

"What was that?" Wyatt whispered.

"I d-d-d-don't kn-kn-know," I whispered back.

The air was electric all around us. A mist of energy invaded our space. It only lasted a couple seconds. We remained frozen, unsure whether to continue.

After a minute or two, we looked at each other warily.

"Think it's gone?" Wyatt asked.

"I don't ev-ev-even know wh-wh-what it-t-t-t was." I replied. "But I w-w-want to get that case out."

We got our hands underneath the case and wrestled it free from the thick dirt that had kept it hidden for decades, maybe longer.

We stood up together, holding the case.

"Not very heavy," I said.

"Lay it on the grass," Wyatt said.

We set it down and for the first time I could clearly see the markings on the front of the case. Across the top was a cluster of unusual symbols.

"That's the same as Dr. Crankenstein's garage!" I shouted.

"Shh!" Wyatt replied, holding his finger to his lips.

"Sorry." I shrunk back and shrugged my shoulders. "I j-j-j-just got a little excited. Don't you think that's interesting?"

"Of course. But it also means it's probably not full of money. Probably just something he buried out here."

"Can't be. This thing looks like it's been buried forever. Dr. Crankenstein only moved in last year. Let's quit yapping about it. Open it up. Let's s-s-s-see what's in it."

Wyatt rubbed the edges of the case all the way around, and looked up at me.

"Ain't no latch on this thing. Not even a keyhole."

"Let me see!" I jerked the case out of his hands and into my lap. The cold slimy dirt on the underside soaked through the legs of my pants. I tilted the case in my hands and stared at the edges. Over and over, I turned it, searching for some kind of access. Wyatt was right. There was no way in.

"That thing's shut t-t-t-tighter than Rockefeller's vault," I whispered.

I rubbed the case all the way around, feeling for anything that might help me pop it open. No matter how hard I rubbed, pressed and stroked, there was no entry to be found.

"Well, that stinks." I flipped it over. The damp dirt clumped on the underside gave me a little hope that I'd still discover a way to open the mysterious case.

"Maybe if we clean it off, we'll find something on this side."

I reached for my t-shirt and started scrubbing the wet dirt off the bottom of the case. Wyatt joined in and soon we began to see markings. Unlike the strange symbols on the other side, these were English letters.

"ARCHIVES…" Wyatt read the first word, which was emblazoned across the center of the case in medieval looking letters. It looked like it was burned into the metal.

We wiped harder, and I started banging on the case to jar more dirt loose.

"OF…" I read.

As we smeared the last of the dirt off the metal, the final word came into view.

"CELESTERIA," Wyatt said.

"Archives of Celesteria," Wyatt mumbled. "What in the world?"

"Or, what out of the world?" I asked, mesmerized by the mysterious case.

"You and your imagination," Wyatt said, shaking his head.

"Are you k-k-kidding," I replied, "This isn't my

imagination. This is real. You're seeing it too. You found it. This is a real life buried treasure."

"Well, it was buried, that's true. But I don't know if it's a treasure," Wyatt said. "We can't open it, so what good is it? Besides we got to finish digging this pit to get Big Harold."

"Really?" My eyes widened as my voice rose. "You really want to still d-d-dig around this pit?" I asked. "We've got some kind of discovery here, a real life mystery. We have to open this c-c-c-case."

"But you can't open it without some kind of hammer or something. Tell you what, I'll help you open it, and you can keep the treasure inside. After we finish digging. This case is cool and all, but Big Harold is going to show up tomorrow morning. I want revenge. You should want it too – just look at your arm."

I looked down at the gauze taped to my forearm. A burgundy blot stained all the way through the frayed cotton mesh.

"You want him to do more of that? Or worse? We need to finish this pit, ok?" Wyatt urged.

"Ok," I said. "Let's get done and get out of here."

I was dying to break into the case, no matter how long or what it took. If that meant helping Wyatt carve out a hole in the ground deep enough for Big Harold, well then, I'd grab a shovel.

We took to digging double time. Silently, side-by-side, we dug without interruption until we were head high in the pit. We were so intent on finishing that we didn't even notice the fading daylight. By the time we pulled ourselves out of the hole, the sky was dark orange and the once mild warmth of late spring was gone. A clammy evening breeze swept across our sweaty bodies as we exited the trench.

"Shoot. It's late!" Wyatt exclaimed.

"No kidding. I didn't even get to v-v-v-visit our hideout." I wriggled into my filthy t-shirt. "Can you carry the shovels for me? I can't carry th-th-them and the case."

"Sure," Wyatt said. "Just give me a second to hide the bucket of fish in the bushes."

"Aren't you afraid a coon or a possum's going to get into it during the night?" I asked.

"Shoot, you're probably right," Wyatt answered. "What'm I gonna do, though? I don't want to tote it back to the house and then back here in the morning. I'll be riling up Big Harold for the chase, and you need to be in position to dump the guts on him."

My eyes scanned the area. We stood between the back of a row of houses and the thick expanse of trees that didn't end until the cemetery. Dr. Crankenstein's back yard was on the other side of the hedges that were just a few feet away. About fifty yards back the way we'd come was the opening to our hideout, tucked discreetly out of sight behind blackberry bushes.

The blackberry bushes were thick and the thorns uninviting, which kept people away. It would be a couple months before the fat berries pulled the branches toward the ground and we could sit and slurp them down until our stomachs ached and our teeth turned purple.

"Let's hide it in our cave," I suggested.

"Ok," Wyatt answered, "but you're going to have to get here earlier to get it out. I won't be here to help you lift it."

I flexed my scrawny arms. "Don't worry about me, I've got the muscles for it."

Wyatt laughed.

"Let's make it a little easier though," I said, "Come on."

We walked away from the freshly widened pit and toward the blackberry bushes. I set the case at my feet.

"Now what?" Wyatt asked.

"Easy," I replied. "Stand back."

I spit on my calloused hands and grabbed the bigger shovel and held it aloft. I ripped into the bushes like a pioneer carving out room for his homestead. After a few minutes of vigorous whacking, we had a clear path to the base of the old oak tree.

I stepped aside and waved my arms. "Ta-da!"

Just beyond my outstretched arms was the familiar tuft of weeds that marked the entrance to our cave.

"Give me the bucket," I said, "and don't let that case out of your sight."

"As you wish," Wyatt replied.

CHAPTER 14

The last time I'd been in our hideout, Charlie was still alive. I took a deep breath and knelt down. Over the years, Wyatt and I had worn a slope smooth that slid from the surface to the open space about ten feet below. I hugged the bucket tightly, ignoring the stench, and inched my way underground.

As I bumped along the damp earth, visibility reduced, I blinked to adjust to the darkness. The fading daylight overhead was strangled by the cluster of tree branches crowding the entrance to our cave. The occasional splash of dead fish juice on my chest wasn't helping.

Just get to the bottom and find the flashlight box.

My feet felt the ground shift from sloped to flat. I was

at the bottom of our cave. I set the bucket of fish guts on the ground and felt in the dark for the old wooden apple boxes near the base of the entrance slide. After fumbling around for a minute, my knee bumped into the thin slats that framed the side of the box.

The clammy air felt especially dense, and the hair on my arms stood on end. As I rummaged in the dark through the wooden box, feeling for one of our trusty flashlights amidst a deflated football, old toys and t-shirts, a flash of green light darted across the wall.

Not now. Not again.

My shaky hands found the rubber handle and clicked on the flashlight. The immediate illumination calmed me.

I shined the bright halogen light around the space. A series of old rusty metal stanchions framed a tunnel that ended about thirty feet away in a pile of dirt. A thick chain double looped around the metal gate that once served as the doorway to an elevator that used to carry miners hundreds of feet below.

I looked along the dirt wall. There was the small patio table stolen from Wyatt's house, alongside a couple of lawn chairs I'd pilfered from my garage.

"You're early but we're running out of time," a sweet airy female voice whispered.

"What? Who's there?" I asked.

I spun around, shining the flashlight wildly in every direction. Its circle of white danced off the mud walls and the metal stanchions. It lit up the silver frame of the lawn chairs, reflecting back into my eyes, temporarily blinding me.

"Tell me who you are! Who's there?" I shouted.

As the word there slipped through my parched lips, the cave lit up with a reddish glow. Like a late summer firefly, it sparked and extinguished in the same instant.

"Atlas? What are you doing?" Wyatt called from above.

I staggered to the entrance of the cave. As I did, the same red glow appeared again. The same one I'd seen from that tree. The same one I'd seen at Charlie's funeral.

"Did you see that?" I hissed to Wyatt.

"See what? I ain't seen nothing. What are you doing down there? We need to get going."

"How long can I dare to wait?" the airy female voice inside the cave said.

"Did you hear that?" I yelled to Wyatt.

"Hear what? I didn't hear nothing besides you banging around like a V-8 with two dead cylinders. I don't see anything neither." Wyatt sounded closer than before. "Are you in la-la land again? Do I got to do everything for us?"

"No...I," I started to reply.

Wyatt's head popped into sight. He hung into the entrance of the cave, shielding his eyes from the flashlight in my hand.

"I could have handled it," I finished. "Where's the

case?"

"What is with you and that case? It's fine. Just relax. Come on, let's go." Wyatt pushed himself back up from the edge.

I scrambled up after him and broke through the surface and stood just outside the hole in the ground. Once again, I saw the red glow. This time it was different. This time I saw the source.

A solitary willow tree stood in the center of Dr. Crankenstein's backyard. It was nearly as tall as his two-story house. Its dangling arms looked like green icicles along the garage roof in the dead of winter. As I stared into the dark, I watched the entire tree radiate with color. A wave of amber, starting at the ground, rose up the trunk and washed through its branches. The leaves glowed a spectacular burnt orange just before the light evaporated into the sky.

"Tell me you saw that," I whispered.

"Saw what?" Wyatt asked. "I don't see nothing but darkness. We need to git home now. We are gonna git in trouble."

"Wyatt. I'm telling you – Dr. Crankenstein's tree just lit up. You didn't see a r-r-r-red light? Nothing?" The wild expression in my face must have startled Wyatt because he stepped back and his eyes widened like he was staring at a ghost.

"I'm sure you saw something, Atlas. But, to be honest,

you're starting to scare me. You're hearing voices, seeing lights in trees – it ain't Christmas, neither – and you're all tied up in knots about that metal box we found in the ground. I'm getting a little worried."

"The case," I replied, "where is it?"

"Right there, where you left it," Wyatt answered.

Night had fallen. Low clouds passed across the moon, blocking most of the natural illumination in the sky. Except for the intermittent red glow that apparently only I could see, we were moving in growing darkness. I looked to where Wyatt pointed.

"The case isn't there," I said, "Come on Wyatt, all you had to do was watch it."

"But, but, it was – " Wyatt stammered.

"There it is," I cut him off. I directed my flashlight along the hedges that separated the back yards from the green space. The white light reflected off the points of the case. The metal brackets shimmered like silver stars.

"Who needs to do everything for us?" I snorted at Wyatt. As I walked toward the case, another light shone from the other side of the hedges.

"Crankenstein's back porch light," I whispered.

I dropped to the ground and crawled toward the hedge that separated the eccentric man's manicured lawn from the wilderness Wyatt and I frequented.

"Shhh!" I replied. The case was just a few feet away, in a spot where ivy had choked a section of hedge from lush green into barren brown. Dry leafless branches were all that filled the space now, the same space through which Dr. Crankenstein's porch light shone brightest.

I don't remember the case being over there, I thought.

No, it definitely was closer to the tree.

I inched along on elbows and knees. I crawled, silent as four o'clock in the morning, toward my newfound treasure.

"Who's there!?" A deep booming voice thundered out, crackling the air like a lightning bolt.

I turned my head and looked back at Wyatt. Like me, he was flat on the ground, frozen with fear.

"I said, who's there?" The bass in Dr. Crankenstein's shout amplified my fright from general fear to absolute frantic.

I lay on the ground, my chin cupped in my hands, my eyes straight ahead. The case rested in the hole in the bushes, tantalizingly close. Over the partial eclipse of the Celesteria container, I saw a silhouette of what appeared to be a giant. Of course, I was looking up from critter level, in the dark, with adrenaline swimming through my body like shallow-water minnows in a thunderstorm.

The silhouette grew larger. Crankenstein was just on the other side of the low hedges.

"Dark is the tide that rises upon forbidden shores. Heavy is the heart that wanders far from home." Dr. Crankenstein was so close I could hear his breathing. His mystical warning guaranteed Wyatt and I would remain still.

"Time to go. But I'm coming back for him soon," someone who was not Dr. Crankenstein said.

It was the voice I'd heard in our hideout, a dainty, almost frail tone that carried a plaintive hope. This was the third time I'd heard it, and it remained disembodied. I didn't move, but I flit my eyes from side to side as rapidly as Dad's Corvette's windshield wipers in a downpour. I didn't see anybody. No one. Nothing.

As I looked ahead once more, the case began to move. It slid along the ground haltingly, like it was being dragged in a losing tug-of-war match. It moved a couple inches then stopped. A couple inches more, scraping along the ground, then paused.

"The restless soul grows weary and the desperate eye waxes teary. Should those around you fall, never abandon your call. When the strength of a thousand warriors begins to wane, the words you speak remain." Dr. Crankenstein said.

He finally walked away from the hedge, back toward his house. The Celesteria case nudged along the ground again. It was about to disappear under the bushes when something jolted me to action. It drew me to itself and I did not resist.

I could not resist.

Quickly but quietly, I stood and stooped and within

a couple blinks, I snatched it with both hands and pulled, expecting resistance. The lack of any rebuff caused me to lose my balance and I tumbled to the ground, case firmly in hand.

I stood to my feet along the forest side of Dr. C's hedges. A recent trim job put the top of the bushes at chest level. I had a clear view of the enormous tree, the rolling yard, and Dr. Crankenstein's backside as he walked away. As he moved through the grass, he favored his right leg. His pronounced limp slowed his progress as he approached the back of the house.

My jaw dropped open. The darkness, the red glow, the strange poetic speech, the gimpy walk. I had been here before. Not here here, exactly. But here. With him.

Charlie's funeral. It was him. Dr. Crankenstein was the strange man who spoke and left. The strange declaration. Those head-scratching words.

As he reached his back porch, he turned. I ducked immediately to the ground. As I squatted behind the bushes, clutching the case, I thought again of his words:

"...though you struggled to find your compass on Earth, *your Atlas remains for the good of us all...*".

"Atlas remains for the good of us all," I whispered. "Atlas remains," I said once more.

"Atlas," Wyatt's voice invaded my thoughts of Dr. C's

eerie prophecy. "Atlas, come on. Let's get out of here."

"Right." I tucked the mystery case under my arm and walked toward Wyatt.

"What was all that?" Wyatt asked as we neared the blackberry bushes.

"I don't know. It's getting weirder, th-th-though." I shined the flashlight down the entrance to our hideout. "The bucket is down there, ready to go."

"All right," Wyatt said before he reached the ground. "Be here at 7:30 in the morning. I'll be running toward the pit with Big Harold chasing me like a vampire after a bloodmobile. As soon as he nears the hole over there," Wyatt pointed back toward Dr. Crankenstein's hedges, "you shower him with the fish guts, he'll stumble and fall into the pit, and we'll have our revenge."

"Ok," I replied. "Now, let's g-g-g-get home."

Wyatt kindly carried the shovels while I remained firmly in control of the closed container. As we hustled out of the woods, a streaking red glow crossed the horizon.

CHAPTER 15

Our garage door was locked.

"Just p-p-p-put the shovels against the side. I'll put them away tomorrow," I told Wyatt.

"Ok." He followed my instructions and turned to walk away. I followed him back down my driveway, holding the case with both hands. He paused as we reached the sidewalk.

"Be there tomorrow. 7:30 AM, ok?" He asked.

"I will, I will. I promise," I said.

"We're going to get Big Harold, good. I can't wait. See you at the pit. And let me know if you open that thing," he smiled as he pointed at the case in my hands.

"Oh, I will. You can c-c-count on it."

Without another word, he turned and jogged toward his home. I hoped his reception would be warmer than the one I was about to receive.

"Where have you been?" Mom asked as I opened the storm door and stepped into our house. Her damp eyes and bright pink nose told me what she'd been doing.

"Don't you know your mother was worried about you?" Dad gruffly clamored from the sitting room. I couldn't see him, which was fine with me.

"Sorry Mom," I whispered. "I was pl-pl-playing with Wyatt and we lost tr-tr-track of time." I reached out my free arm to give her a half-hug.

"What is that?" she asked. She leaned away from me and cast a skeptical gaze at the dirty object under my arm. Her eyes then traced my entire body and returned to my face.

"You're filthy!" she exclaimed. "What have you been doing?"

"I was digging with Wyatt in the woods. You know, just having fun."

"Don't you think there's better ways to spend your time than making mud pies like a toddler?" Dad piled on without joining us in the entryway.

"Yes, D-D-D-Dad," I mumbled.

I didn't have it in me to engage in another passive aggressive argument with him. I just wanted to get up to my room, lock my door, and figure out how to open the inexplicable metal phenomenon we had unearthed.

"Understand this, Atlas," Mom put her arms around me despite the fact that I looked like a Dickensian street urchin. My mud drenched clothing and my scratch laced flesh would make anyone think I'd spent the day either hopping boxcars or laying the train tracks that they rode on.

I was a mess. Mom's eyes saw right through it.

"You're my only boy now. *Our only boy.*" As she said the words, her voice trembled and her grip tightened. "I just love you so much Atlas," she whispered in my dirt-caked ear.

"I know Mom. I'm sorry."

"Go on. Get yourself cleaned up and get to bed."

She released me and stepped aside. As I passed her, I shifted the case to my left and started up the stairs. I paused and looked back at Mom, who was vainly trying to brush away the residue that remained on her clothes after our embrace.

"I love you too, Mom," I whispered.

As I reached the top of the stairs, I heard my father's voice. I should have ignored it and went into my room, but his hushed tone held me. I eavesdropped, silently wedging my skinny rump into the corner between the banister and the wall next to Hannah's door. I peeked into her cotton-candy-princess-land of a room. Her gentle breathing gave the impression of contented sleep. She was, as Marty would say, "out like a bank robber in a silk suit." Not everything Marty said made sense.

"I'm worried, Meredith," Dad whispered in the hallway below.

"Why, Preston? Because he's different from Charlie? *Because he's not like you?*" Mom's voice crackled like dry kindling in an inferno as she defended me.

"He's doing what he knows to do," she continued, "maybe even what he's meant to do."

"I know, Meredith. I know everyone has their own path. I just want Atlas to find a path that fits the *real world*. He's not a kid anymore, and with Charlie gone, he's the oldest. He needs to grow up. Maybe we've been too easy on him."

"What do you want him to do? He makes good grades. He has a nice friend, Wyatt. He doesn't cause trouble. What is so wrong?"

"I just don't think he has much ambition, that's all. He was out digging in the woods all evening." Dad returned to his point. The only point he ever had, as far as my life was concerned.

"When I was twelve, I was working. I was learning how to be a man. You don't think there's better ways for him to spend his time?"

"You had to work. I'm sorry you didn't get much of a childhood. But your life isn't his life," Mom answered, "I've got an idea, Preston, if you're so worried about him doing something worthwhile, why don't you take him to work with you? Take him to your office and give him something to do."

"Are you nuts?" Dad scoffed. "I can't take him to work. He can barely talk without stuttering at home, much less out in public. He would mumble around all tongue-tied. It would just be an embarrassment."

Mom's voice roared in response.

"Are you nuts!? That's your response to me? His mother?" Mom lit into him with more fire and brimstone than Brother Westler's best sermon. "You better hold your tongue, Mr. Bigshot! What is your problem!? You're talking about your son. Your only son now. You're ashamed of your son – a boy who has done nothing but love and obey us. A boy who has a little trouble talking and you want to hide him from your co-workers? Be a man, Preston! *Or don't be anything to us!*"

I tilted my head back. My eyes filled with tears as I heard Mom's thudding footsteps go out the door and across the front porch.

"Oh my God," I whispered.

"God!" I heard from below. "Come on Meredith, come back here."

The room was silent.

Go after her, Dad.

"What is going on?" Dad's voice carried up the staircase. "I'm doing everything I know to do. How am I

supposed to know how to be a father? I never had one."
Staccato breathing followed by a deep sigh and genuine
sniffles echoed up the hardwood stairs. Dad was crying.

"Charlie's gone. Meredith's run out the door. God,
God, God."

My heart raced and a gulp caught in my throat. I had
never heard Dad talk like this.

"Umm. I don't know if you're real, God," Dad's halting
voice continued, "I know I'm not a church-going man. But
right now, I'm losing my mind. The walls are caving in. I
don't know how to connect with Atlas. I try. Nothing comes
out right. I've already lost my first son. I don't want to lose
my entire family. Help me. Please. I'm lost and I'm afraid
I'll never figure out how to find my way."

A scraping sound, then a thud, followed his earnest
plea as he slid to the floor below.

Tears trickled down my face as I sat on the ground.

A soft clap sound came from Hannah's room.

Clap. Clap.

I rubbed my eyes.

Clap.

"Atlas?" Hannah whispered. "I'm clapping my hands."

I slowly stood and walked into Hannah's room. Sure
enough, she was laying in her bed, arms outstretched. I
knelt on the carpet and wrapped my arms around her,
spilling dirt onto her rainbow bedspread and spilling tears
onto her puffy pink pillows.

"You remembered," she whispered.

"I'll never forget," I replied.

Hannah buried her head into my chest and latched onto my shoulders with all her might. I pulled her close. I could feel her heart beating against my chest. I guess I hadn't really thought about how she was feeling. Sad how easy it is to be selfish.

After more than a few seconds of deep squeezing, I released my grip and tiptoed into the hall, grabbing the case. I shut my door behind me as quietly as a spy behind enemy lines and placed the case on the foot of my bed and tunneled under the covers. For at least thirty minutes, I lay there, cycling through sobs and whimpers. The next thing I knew the red glow of the bedside clock read 7:00 AM.

CHAPTER 16

My sheets were caked with dirt. I had dozed off in my filthy clothes. Even my shoes were still on my feet. I bolted up in my bed. It wasn't just the red LED of the clock. My entire room was bathed in an eerie red, like someone had put a giant strip of plastic film from old 3-D glasses on everything.

I shut my eyes hard. I'm just dreaming, I thought.

I opened my eyes. The pale crimson glow remained.

I'm not dreaming.

I stood to my feet. Clumps of dirt dropped onto the Corvette throw rug beside my bed.

"I specialize in imagination. But, this is too much. What is the deal?" I said aloud. After everything that had happened in the past month, I genuinely expected an answer.

And an answer came. Well, not exactly an answer, but a sound. A sound emanated from the end of my bed. It was faint, but I could hear it. Lyrical and lilting, it entranced me. It was symphonic and contained the soulful sounds of bagpipes, the flitting flight of a violin's dancing strings, the crystal clarity of a perfectly tuned piano and the rhythmic thump of a solitary drum.

I dropped to my knees and looked for the source. Through the overhanging blanket and the bed frame, I saw it. The case was lying open on the ground just past the end of my bed.

I scrambled and stumbled across the floor until I reached the mysterious box. The red light grew brighter and the rapturous melody intensified as I knelt down.

A kaleidoscope of light and sound flooded my senses. My skin warmed and my insides trembled. The open case was trimmed in gray suede. There were no compartments or pockets. A thin cord of translucent fiber barely thicker than a spider's web ran along the single hinge. The light came from it, or through it.

One side of the case hosted a rectangular crystal. It reminded me of the insides of some of the rocks they'd pull up from the coalmines, like a soup of color in a stone bowl. Purplish-gray with white streaks, diamond speckles and black smears all through it.

The other side held the oldest book I've ever seen. The cover was so worn and musty I wouldn't have been surprised if it'd sprouted moss. Burgundy and dark brown with yellowed lettering etched in it, the binding was a fabric that felt like leather mixed with rubber. It was tight and had a dull shine from decades, maybe centuries of being rubbed, held, and caressed.

The sounds – make that song, no doubt it was a song – rose in my ears and filled my heart.

Above the melody, above the strains of strings and the cries of cymbals, rose that voice once again; the tender, mournful, pleading feminine voice that I'd heard the night before. But now, it didn't speak. It sang. It sang with passion. It sang with the heaviness of a burden my naïve youth couldn't yet comprehend, although in the past few weeks I'd come close.

Like dense fog in the early morning, it was startling and impenetrable. It rose in a language not my own.

I leaned closer to the case. I already saw, heard, and felt. Now I breathed, absorbing every inch, every ounce, every scent. In the same instant, this completely foreign thing felt like home. A new light joined the red, a soft glow from the stone. It was inviting and soothing.

I reached out to touch it but was rebuked by a shock that sent me reeling and rolling across my bedroom. It stung me harder than when I'd leaned against the electric fence around Uncle Huey's pigpen a few years earlier.

"Ouch," I muttered, speaking for the first time since the sound began. "Must be some kind of force field."

I crawled back toward the case. The song intensified as I approached. It beckoned me. It drew me in. I sensed the pain and desperation of the singer. I wanted to help, if only I knew how.

I lay down and studied the stone once more. I couldn't see anything but I wasn't going to touch it. Not after that shock.

Maybe the book?

I studied it closely. It looked harmless enough, but then again, so had the jolting crystal.

Slowly, I moved my arm until my hand hovered above the ancient text. At the same time, the song reached a crescendo. An explosion of sound and light enveloped me and to my great delight, as I gingerly placed my hand on the book, no shock came.

I scooped the book from the case like it was a pile of precious stones from a treasure chest. As I leaned back and sat on my feet, cradling the book, the music began to fade. The red light dimmed. All that remained was a muted voice, now acapella, singing lightly and limited, as though it was restrained or even choked by something I couldn't see.

The sounds, which had been unfamiliar the entire morning, suddenly became clear. They were recognizable. They were the most familiar sounds of all, at least for me.

"At last, At last," I heard her sing.

Was that it? At last?

I leaned closer and shut my eyes once again, quieting every input and impulse save the tiny whisper I'd first heard in the tree house.

"At last...Atlas."

"Atlas, At last," I heard over and over again.

My name. Or is it?

"Atlas, Atlas. At last."

"What?" I finally asked. "What can I do? Do you need help?"

"You're going to need help." A different voice answered. A much louder voice. A very familiar voice. "You're going to need help if you don't hurry, Atlas. It's time for school." My mother called from beyond my closed bedroom door.

The singing voice was gone. The light was gone. I looked around. My room was a disaster area. I looked down at my polluted clothing. I was a disaster area.

"School." I replied. "Of course."

Mom banged on my door. "Come on Atlas, it's seven-thirty. You need to get to the bus stop in five minutes."

"Seven-thirty!" I shouted. "Seven-thirty! Crap! It's seven-thirty!"

Seven-thirty. Be there tomorrow. Seven-thirty in the morning. I heard Wyatt's voice in my head from the night before, instructing me to be in position for Big Harold's comeuppance.

Wyatt. He's all by himself.

I slumped onto my back and stared at the ceiling.
The book slid from my hands onto the floor. I jumped
to my feet, and was just about to open the door when I
remembered the book and the case, lying on my floor.

I hurried to the case and slid it under my bed. I pulled
my covers so they hung all around the sides of the bed and
touched the floor, concealing my treasure. I grabbed the
book. It was large, the size of the old family Bible Meemaw
kept on the coffee table, the one with the illustrations that
looked like oil paintings sprinkled throughout. I always
liked the stoic picture of Daniel in the lions' den, somehow
not getting eaten. He seemed so brave, facing those deadly
beasts.

"I hope Wyatt's braver than I am prompt," I said while
stuffing the book into my backpack, crushing another set of
incomplete assignments into wrinkled oblivion.

I swung my backpack over my shoulder and flew out
of my room, skipping most of the steps as I bounded to the
first floor of our house.

"There's toast in the kitchen," Mom yelled from
Hannah's room.

"Come on and join me for breakfast, son," Dad called
from the kitchen.

"Wish I could, Dad," I replied, "can't miss the bus."

The front door banged open as I streaked out of the
house and skipped down the steps of the front porch. By

the time I reached the sidewalk, the race was on. This race wasn't timed. It was a race against time.

CHAPTER 17

The bus stop was quieter than a blank page. Instead of the usual silliness and occasional flirting, there was nothing. Correction, there was nobody.

I continued sprinting, past the familiar hydrant. Out of the corner of my eye, I could see the bus. The big yellow mechanical beast was chugging down the hill a couple blocks up, Ms. Turpentine's unmistakable heft filling most of the flat square front window.

With each pounding stride of my dirty shoes on cement, my fear for Wyatt rose. My backpack boomeranged against my body repeatedly, each thud against my back a reminder of the secret book weighing me down as I hurried to rescue my friend.

Ahead of me, just shy of the tree line that separated the neighborhood from the woods, several classmates were running

"Go Wyatt, go!" Some were yelling.

"Big Harold, fat butt can't run!" another voice cried out.

I burst onto the trail we'd traveled the night before, just behind the cajoling crowd, legs flying, arms flailing, as the leaves overhead shaded the early morning sun. My vision blurred while my eyes adapted to the darker surroundings.

A few blinks and I was acclimated. On the trail before me, a Rushmorian assemblage of heads blocked my view. A cluster of tan and white bodies clogged the path like Meemaw's hash browns in the sink drain.

"Outta my way!" I yelled as I nosed into the widest slit available. I wedged between Maxine Jacobs and her whiny sidekick, Marjorie Jenkins.

"Hey, watch it," Marjorie yelled.

I twisted just so, intentionally banging Marjorie's shoulder with my heavy backpack.

"Ouch! You're a jerk, Atlas Forman!"

I ignored the whiner and sprinted into the open path.

I can get there. I can still make it.

"Atlas, now!" Wyatt screamed from somewhere on the path ahead of me.

Or not...

I couldn't see him yet. I was not going to make it up to the pit to dump the trout entrails and eyeballs on Big Harold. Which meant he wouldn't stumble and slip into the pit. Which meant he wouldn't be trapped. Which meant…

"Atlas!" Wyatt's shrill voice urgently pleaded. "Atlas!"

"Ain't no Atlas here," a deep, nearly breathless voice panted in response.

Big Harold.

"I'm coming!" I shrieked.

"You ain't gonna do nothing, punk," Big Harold answered through the trees. "And Wyatt's gonna pay big time. Like a thick roll of Benjamins in a brown paper bag."

The clearing in the woods just ahead let me know I was near the pit. Near my best friend.

"Hang on Wyatt!" I yelled.

"Too late, loser. Boom goes the dynamite!" Big Harold shouted.

"No, no," I moaned.

Wyatt was hanging on, all right. Just not the way I'd hoped. I reached the opening where the big revenge was supposed to go down. The only thing going down was Wyatt.

Big Harold had him by the neck with both hands. Wyatt dug into Harold's forearms, his feet dangling and kicking against the bully's tank of a body.

Beneath Wyatt's swinging legs was the trench we'd intended for Big Harold. Somehow, he'd caught Wyatt and was preparing to dispose of my only friend.

"Let him go!" I yelled.

Big Harold grinned the expectant grin of a toddler about to open a pile of birthday presents.

"As you wish, grape licorice," he replied.

With that, he released Wyatt. Down Wyatt fell, straight into the hole. Straight into the spot intended for our enemy. Straight into the pit that would have held Big Harold, if only I'd been there a few minutes sooner.

"Dang it," I whispered and hung my head, trying to decide if I was going to be foolish enough to fight the lug that'd just ruined my morning and maybe my only friendship. I didn't get much time to think.

"You're next, Forman," Big Harold said.

Over the ground, a dark spot rolled across the grass. Harold was rumbling toward me, like an overweight bull seeing red.

"What's happening? Where'd Wyatt go?" I heard the voices of the other students behind me.

The lookie-loos shouted out questions, their taunts fading as Big Harold approached. The closer people get to danger, the more true character is revealed.

My character, also, was about to get stripped as bare and pale as a Thanksgiving turkey. Like that dead bird, I didn't have wings, but as Big Harold steamed closer, I decided to fly.

I turned to flee and got about three steps down the

runway before colliding with the get-along-gang. Down I went, elbows and knees banging with my rubber-necking classmates.

As I fell to the ground, my backpack somersaulted into the weeds.

All I could think about was the book. Escape was important, but there was no way I was leaving without my sacred possession.

I clawed across the tangled rabble of students, pulling on Mike Green's slender arm. I jerked my leg out from under Maxine's tie-dyed satchel. A clump of Marjorie's red curls was twisted around my watch. I jerked it free, bringing more than a few of those blazing orange fibers along for the ride.

As Marjorie whined, "Atlas, you are so clumsy", I clambered to my feet and made for my backpack.

"Your turn scrawny loser," Big Harold yelled. "Time for you to take a dump – I mean, for me to dump you in the dirt toilet with your crappy friend."

My stumble had given Harold time to reach me. He closed in fast. I reached for my backpack. As I grabbed it, a mounded shadow appeared on the grass around me.

"Where you think you're going?" Big Harold asked.

The question hit my eardrums at the same time as two beefy hands hit my ears. Ringing echoed in my head and the puffs of air forced into my ear canals squished my brain.

Big Harold grabbed me by the neck and jerked me

around before I could swing my bag over my shoulder. My hands clung to it tighter than the fit of my funeral suit. Now face-to-face, I stared at his dark brown eyes. Soulless or mindless, I couldn't tell, but either way, there was no redeeming quality in that dull stare. My backpack provided a shield of sorts, a buffer between his sweltering girth and my squirming gangle.

"I'm just going to the b-b-bus. We g-g-g-got to get to school on t-t-time, you know," I offered.

"No you're not. You ain't so hot. You're a little ball of snot." Big Harold smirked. He slapped his hands against my ears again; so hard I thought my brains were going to explode through my nose.

"Ow! Come on, man, ease up," I squeaked.

He pressed all the harder and began leading me toward the pit. I could see Wyatt's arms and hands, reaching up, grabbing turf as he tried to hoist himself out.

"Don't go anywhere, Wyatt," Harold called out. "I'm bringing you a friend. Y'all can play in that pit like a couple of – what was it you called me the other day, Atlas?"

"Nothing, I didn't call you n-n-nothing," I whimpered.

The onlookers stood far to the side, none trying to help. As we passed by them, Big Harold continued talking, clearly reveling in his rant.

"Fairy? Was that it?" He asked, nearly lifting my feet off the ground as he bounced me toward the waiting shaft where Wyatt's head was now bobbing near the edge, elbows digging into the soft ground as he reached for an exposed tree root to pull himself out.

"Fruity? Maybe? Hey fruity Wyatt! I got a friend for you. Don't be climbing out now. The fun's just begun!"

Big Harold flung me to the ground. I landed face down and skidded to the edge of the hole. My backpack bounced forward, slamming my head into the ground. As my mouth and nose filled with clods of mud and grass, I saw Wyatt's familiar cowlick poking up through the chickweed in front of me. Another two lunges and he'd be out.

I may not have been able to spare him the first attack from Big Harold, but as I spit the sludgy clay from my mouth, I determined to help him avoid the second one.

I rolled onto my back just as Harold stepped over me. His ample ankles, encased in military surplus boots, squeezed my thighs together. He leaned over, staring at me. I held his stare while sliding my left hand out to feel for the nylon handle of my backpack.

"Not so fast. Ha! Dead. Now. Boy." Harold barked. He grabbed my backpack and tossed it into the hole.

He reached down and shook me by the shoulders. I saw stars and then, Harold's lumpy cheeks and bushy eyebrows were awash in red. Either I was concussed, or the tree behind us was glowing like the night before.

"Like I said, fruity fairy boy, your friend needs some company."

He yanked me off the ground and spun me around. The tree was glowing that strange amber light. Everything was swirling. I looked down at my backpack, so small at the bottom of the pit.

My book.

"You won't be calling me names anymore, now will ya!?" Harold yelled.

He shoved me with all his might. I nearly broke in half as I flew forward. My head snapped back as I hit the far side of the hole just as Wyatt's feet scrambled over the edge. The last thing I saw over the broken line of dirty dandelions rimming the edge of the pit was Wyatt, standing to his feet.

My face slammed against the side of the pit, and everything went dark.

CHAPTER 18

I heard voices overhead, a hodge-podge of sound. I couldn't discern who was speaking, but there was more than one.

"At simp flats blay wey leerie onslo."

"Terra flit dulsera crantay."

I'm delirious. I'm probably in the hospital.

"Floo moo sleen wamsora."

Or the morgue.

Ribbons of pink light danced across the sky as I fluttered my eyelids. The air smelled of burning leaves.

"No, you're not dead." That airy soft voice I'd heard repeatedly in the past twenty-four hours answered.

Wake up, Atlas, I thought.

I felt cool grass tickling my hands. My head was pounding.

"Where am I?" I asked.

"Where you belong," the sweet voice replied. "At the crossroads of hope and desperation. Where danger and destiny collide."

"What? Who are you?" I asked.

"My name is Talia," the voice replied.

"Where are you?" I asked.

I turned my head from side to side. I was flat on my back, just beside the open pit where I'd landed face first moments, or minutes or maybe hours before. A large dark bundle lay on the ground to my left.

My backpack.

The book.

I reached for it. A shooting pain erupted in my ribs and crackled along my arm. I grabbed my side and slid along the ground toward my backpack.

"Stand up, please." Talia commanded.

"Stand up?" I asked, incredulous.

"Yes. We need to go."

"Where? And, I still can't see you. Where are you?"

"I'm over here," Talia replied.

I turned my head in the direction of her voice.

"Here I am," she said.

"Where?" I pushed myself up, wincing as the pain in my side intensified.

I leaned on my elbows and blinked repeatedly.

"Here," she whispered.

She had the voice of a girl. But when she finally came into view, what I saw was not a girl. Well, at least not a girl from Earth.

Right in front of me, hovering over my chest, was the tiniest person I'd ever seen. I say person because she looked human, except she was no more than eighteen inches tall. She had all the necessary parts to be human: two arms, two legs, hands and feet and a face with a nose, two eyes and a mouth.

I slid back. I gulped and sputtered.

"Who, err, what are you?"

"My name is Talia, daughter of Davner, of the house of Brunestilla, in the kingdom of Celesteria. I am an Apharmari. I am a child of the Necessary Dream. I am here to take you to the battle."

Celesteria. The book.

I pulled my backpack close to my body.

"Battle? What battle?" I asked.

"Please stand."

I didn't stand. I just stared.

Her dark wavy hair fell long and full to just below her waist. Her cheeks, speckled with light brown freckles, were a constellation of light brown stars under her shimmering blue eyes. She wore a lavender smock, trimmed with gold lace. Ornate symbols were woven into the trim. They looked like the hieroglyphs on the metal case, same as on Crankenstein's garage.

A plain silver pendant, which looked like a hollowed-out bottle stopper, hung around her neck, suspended by a silver chain half the width of dental floss.

She floated closer to my face.

"It's time. Please stand," she implored.

I elbowed myself to a seated position. For the first time since I woke up, I noticed that I was not in the pit. I flung my head around. Behind me were the woods where Wyatt and I often played, just as they always were. Up the way were the blackberry bushes that marked our hideout entrance. On my right, the low hedges along Dr. Crankenstein's backyard.

"Stand up," she ordered.

I rolled onto my knees and slowly pushed myself to standing. As I slung my bag over my shoulder, I continued to survey the area.

The trees looked fuller and denser than before. The air buzzed with an electric hum, as it had the night before. The red glow from the enormous tree flashed.

"Making friends is like fishing," Marty used to say. "And fishing is like making friends. It all begins with a proper introduction."

Don't know why that came to me, but I responded as if Marty was standing next to me, rubbing his greasy gray beard.

"Hello, my name is Atlas Forman. It's nice to meet you."

I extended my hand.

She didn't shake my hand, which was impossible, given our extreme difference in size.

Like a leaf with legs, she fluttered and came to a rest on my now open palm. Her touch was weightless, but was as soon as her foot made contact with my skin, a radiating energy flooded my body.

"Hello Atlas," she replied. "Sometimes I forget about the customs of your world. Please forgive me, but time is very short. Death is all around. Life hangs by a thread. The Rephiamasts have again broken our fortifications. We suffer. And when the Apharmari suffer, Earth suffocates."

"I'm sorry, umm, Tabitha?" I asked.

"Talia."

"I'm sorry Talia. Where are you from?" I asked.

"I'm from Celesteria, as I said. Please come help us."

"Help you with what?"

She stepped up onto my wrist. Her eyes glittered and flashed as another red burst filled the air around us.

"And what's with that tree?" I blurted out.

"The answers to all your questions are in there." She pointed at my bag.

"In the book?" I asked.

"Yes. Your discovery of the Archives was not a mistake. Premature, to be sure, but not accidental. Nothing is accidental." Talia flit away from my hand and bobbed in the air, near my eyes. Her eyes were set wide but her gaze was tight.

"But you can't read it yet. Not without this," she said.

She clapped her hands together, mere inches from my eyes. A wisp of green fog floated from her hands. It rushed into my eyes, like tears in reverse.

"What was that?" I gasped and coughed.

"Your eyes will be opened. Your destiny will be known. Anything is possible for those who dream. Not just dream, but have the courage to speak their dreams. Turn the pages to enter the real world. All of this – every little bit – is meant to become."

"These riddles. Puzzles, confusion and mystery. You're like Dr. Crankenstein at Charlie's funeral and the other night when we found the case."

I looked beyond her at the empty expanse of grass in his backyard. I stared at the large glowing tree.

"What is this all about? Why did you come to me? How did you get here?" The questions rolled from my tongue as I returned my gaze to her face. She had a thin nose and full lips, which framed her perfect white teeth like pearls couched in a rose petal. Her ears curled at the tips and folded over into a tail-like appendage, which was tucked into her thick shimmering dark hair.

Beautiful hair. Like Aamilah's.
Aamilah.

School!

"I came to protect my Renall Benji...um, you call him Harold. Big Harold. When I realized you were the Ekyllion, the one, I couldn't resist. I just had to..." Talia began.

"School!" I interrupted her. "I've got to get to school!"

"School?" she asked.

"Yes," I replied. "School. The place where I go every day to learn. It's where my friends, Wyatt and Aamilah, are. Well, Wyatt is my friend...er, was. After this fiasco, maybe not."

"School is secondary. Life is primary. It was for life that I came, and it is to rescue life that we must go. Now."

"Talia!" a deep but feminine voice shouted from Dr. Crankentein's yard.

Talia stopped bobbing. She froze in the air. Her face turned redder than the burst of light from the strange tree. She stared at me, her eyes giant pools of fear. She looked like I felt when I got sent to Principal Wilkins's office.

"Talia, return at once!" The voice ordered. "Contact is forbidden. You are in direct violation of the primary Apharmari Observances!"

In a blink, the tiny fluttering girl spun high overhead, twirling and twisting until she was just a streak of lavender and green.

I blinked and she was gone.

CHAPTER 19

I stood alone. The energy in the air was gone. Only then did I realize how tightly I was gripping my backpack. My left hand was numb from being wedged between the strap and my shoulder. My head throbbed.

How long have I been here?

How did I get out of the pit?

I turned slowly in a circle. I surveyed the area. The pit was there, just twenty or so feet behind me.

"Atlas!"

A voice called my name from the trail back to the street.

"Yes?" I called back.

"Atlas, are you ok?"

"I th-th-think s-s-s-so."

The overhanging branches parted and there stood Aamilah. In the middle of the path, her big brown eyes curtained by her lustrous black hair. She grinned and sped up.

"I was on the bus when a bunch of the kids came running out of the woods," she said. "Miss Turpentine told me to stay on the bus but when Marjorie said you were trapped in a hole, I got worried that something bad happened. I don't know what I'd do if you were...umm, I mean, I'm really glad you're ok."

I stood up as straight as I could as Aamilah reached me. I cleared my throat and brushed off my shirt.

"You're bleeding," Aamilah said. She brushed my cheek with the back of her hand. My knees buckled but I kept my feet.

"R-r-r-real-ly-ly-ly?"

Say something cool. Be strong, I told myself.

"Yes, you are. And it looks like you've got a black eye." Aamilah stepped back and thumped her hands against her hips. She cocked her head and stared at me.

"What the heck happened, Atlas?" She asked.

"W-w-w-well, uhh, Wyatt and me set up th-th-this tr-tr-trap to g-g-g-g-g-get B-B-Big Harold. But I was l-l-l-late."

"Wyatt and Big Harold?" Aamilah looked around. She looked over my shoulder. "I don't see Wyatt or Big Harold," she said. "And he's hard to miss."

"They aren't on th-th-the b-b-b-bus?"

"No. They never came to the stop. At least not before I left. And Miss Turpentine told me she was leaving and it wasn't her fault if I got in trouble."

"They aren't on th-th-the b-b-b-bus?"

"That's what I said. Atlas, you should probably get your mom to take you to the doctor. You look pretty banged up."

She stepped closer to me and reached out to take my arm. She led me down the path, away from the pit. Away from the glowing tree. Away from whatever was happening in that strange place.

As we walked into the shade of the foliage, I thought I saw the red glow once again.

"There! D-d-d-did you s-s-see that?" I asked, nudging Aamilah's arm, which was locked in mine.

She turned to look.

"See what?"

"Th-th-the r-r-r-red light. F-fr-from the tr-tree."

"No. What light? What tree?"

We stopped walking as Aamilah turned to face me. Our arms separated. A smattering of sunlight forced its way through the leaves above us, creating a disco ball effect on her face and shirt.

She is so pretty. Oh my gosh.

I should show her the book.

My thoughts were a rambling mess.

"What is going on with you, Atlas?" She rubbed her arms as she spoke. "You seem nice but sometimes it's like you're in another world. It's not normal. I'm not trying to be mean but…"

"I know," I mumbled.

And here we were, starting to connect. Whatever. I'm keeping the book to myself.

No one's going to believe me.

Just get home.

I looked at the ground. A swarm of ants carried half a bee carcass across an exposed chunk of gnarled tree root.

"What about y-y-you?" I finally asked.

"What about me?" Aamilah replied.

"Well, you're diff-diff-differ-different, too."

"Really Atlas? You're going with the racial stuff? I thought you were better than that – better than the rest of the country hicks around here." She huffed and stepped back. She tripped and stumbled over the ant-covered tree root.

I grabbed her arm to help her gain her balance. "No, not th-th-that k-k-kind of different," I replied.

She gripped my forearm tightly and steadied herself.

We were closer than we'd ever been. Face to face. I'd imagined this moment many times but never like this.

"I mean you are d-d-deeper, you kn-kn-know? Like th-th-there is more to you than j-j-j-just the usual st-st-

134

stuff. It's like you have li-li-lived longer or th-th-thought more deeply than the other kids. I noticed r-r-r-right away. The f-f-f-first time we talked."

"How so?" Her voice softened but her eyes remained skeptical.

"You n-n-n-n..."

"What? You can say it, Atlas. Whatever it is." She smiled, just a little.

"You never made f-f-fun of me. You l-l-laughed w-w-with me. Not at me."

"Well, you are funny," she whispered. "Funny looking," she laughed.

"Oh really?" I shot back. "Speaking of l-l-looking. Wh-What ab-b-b-bout how you were st-st-staring at me during Ch-Ch-Cha-Charlie's funeral?"

I finally said it; what I'd wondered since that day, now out in the open for her to respond.

"I was sad for you, Atlas. I'm sorry if you felt like I was staring at you. But then, you kept looking back at me, so I thought it would make you feel better to see a friendly face. Atlas, I want to be your friend."

Friend. Yippee.

"Thanks," I replied.

I looked down the path at the circle of light coming through the opening at the end of the woods. The street wasn't far away.

I started walking.

"Let's ju-ju-ju-just get going. At least I can g-g-get cr-cr-credit for a half day of school."

"Half day?" Aamilah asked. She jogged to join me.

We reached the edge of the tree line and walked into the sun-drenched sidewalk. The temperature was probably already eighty degrees.

"Yeah."

"Atlas, it's only been five or ten minutes since I left the bus. If your mom can drive us, we'll be on time for school."

CHAPTER 20

Mom was less upset than I'd expected, but that probably had a lot to do with Aamilah's presence. Mom cleaned me off, bandaged my cheek and whistled at the fried-egg shaped bruise on my right side.

"Well, Atlas, it's been a rough stretch for all of us," she said as she tossed me a clean t-shirt. "I sure hope things turn around soon."

"Me too." I ducked into the small bathroom in the front hallway and took off my dirty shirt. I winced as I tried to put on the new t-shirt without raising my arms too high. Now was as good a time as any to inspect my appearance. I turned my eyes to the mirror above the sink but my ears stayed attentive to the conversation in the hallway.

"You're new here, right? What's your name?" Mom asked.

"Yes ma'am. We moved here last year. I'm Aamilah."

"Do you have any classes with Atlas?"

"Yes. We are in math and history together."

Science class too, I thought.

I leaned closer to the mirror and studied my thin face. My eyes were bloodshot. The purple bruise on my cheek made my skin look as pale as a full moon. I gingerly tapped my cheek.

Ouch.

"How did you end up with him this morning?" Mom asked.

"He got in a disagreement with a couple guys from school. I just came to make sure he was ok," Aamilah discreetly replied.

"I'm sure Atlas wouldn't be getting in a fight. He's a good boy. He's cute too, don't you think?" Mom asked, with no discretion whatsoever.

I cleared my throat and opened the door.

Mom stood near the staircase railing, holding a bundle of anti-drunk driving propaganda. Aamilah leaned toward the front door, with a look that said "get me out of here."

"Ok, ready to take us to school, Mom?" I asked.

"Meemaw is going to take you." She turned to me and held up her pack of materials. "I've got a meeting to get to."

Mom stepped into the sitting room, leaving Aamilah and me in the hallway. I glanced at Aamilah and shrugged my shoulders.

"Parents," I whispered.

She nodded.

"Meemaw!" Mom yelled. "Need you to do me a favor!"

I wanted to bury my face in my hands. Bad enough that Aamilah used the 'friend' word on me in the woods. Now, my Mom was doing her best to guarantee I never became anything more than friend material in Aamilah's eyes.

"Face things head on," Marty's voice filled my thoughts, "which makes sense since your face is on the front of your head."

So, I took Marty's advice. Instead of burying my face, I looked at Aamilah's. She was grinning with the knowing smirk of a kid who'd been embarrassed by her parents as much as I any other kid. I smiled back.

"Meemaw! Turn off the radio!" Mom shouted. She returned from the sitting room and looked at Aamilah.

"Sorry, dear. I would love to take you all to school. It would give Aamilah and me a chance to have some girl talk. But, I'm leading the group in today's meeting. We're going to put an end to drunk driving in this county." Mom whipped her head back and shouted before Aamilah could reply.

"Meemaw!"

"I'm coming, I'm coming," thundered Meemaw's raspy bass from somewhere deep in the kitchen. "Don't lose your religion. I'll be right there."

I grabbed my backpack. The weight of the book required me to heave it pretty good to toss it over my shoulder.

"Whatcha got in there, son?" Mom asked.

"I'm here. What do ya need?" Meemaw asked as she lumbered into the hallway.

For a moment the four of us stood there, Mom eyeing my backpack, Meemaw eyeing Mom, me staring at the front door and Aamilah staring at the three of us.

"Hello, Meredith. Is your hearing going along with your sense of style?" Meemaw asked.

"What's that supposed to mean?" Mom glared back.

"If the shoe fits, especially those candlestick heels you're wearing. Mercy." Meemaw snaked a pack of smokes from her handbag and nudged me in the side. "You ready to go Atlas?"

I gripped my backpack.

"Yes, Meemaw, I'm ready."

She was halfway through the front door.

"Allrighty, then. Atlas, get in my car." She pointed at Aamilah, who was mere inches away. "And you, Atlas's girlfriend, come on, let's get y'all to school."

"We'll talk more when you get home, Atlas," Mom said as she walked down the hall toward the garage.

"Yes Mom."

I hadn't been in the back of Meemaw's car since Charlie's funeral. The vinyl covered seat and the cigarette stench was definitely not the atmosphere I'd pictured for spending quality time with Aamilah.

"So, kids, where can I take ya?" Meemaw joked as she revved the engine. A couple pops resounded from the exhaust.

"J-j-j-just school, Meem-m-m-maw," I replied as I slipped the seat belt over my shoulder and mouthed "sorry" to Aamilah.

She giggled.

"What's so-s-s-so fu-fu-funny?" I asked.

She shook her head and batted her eyes. Her shiny hair danced across her tan cheek and chin.

"Sorry I can't play no rap music," Meemaw yelled from the front seat. "This beauty," she patted the dash, expelling a puff of dust into the air, "might have seen better days, but she still gets my favorite FM country station. Listen to this."

With that, my grandmother cranked the old plastic black knob and raised the volume by a factor of ten.

"Maybe I didn't love you
Quite as often as I could have
And maybe I didn't treat you
Quite as good as I should have"

"Nobody shoots straighter or sings purer than Willie, huh kids?"

Aamilah and I stared out our windows as Meemaw raised the awkwardness to new heights.

"Little things I should have said and done
I just never took the time
You were always on my mind
You were always on my mind"

"I guess those days are gone," Meemaw said, mostly to herself. "We had some fun didn't we Jeff?"

Meemaw tapped the faded black and white photo booth picture tucked into the gas gauge behind her steering wheel.

"You're always on my mind," she said as she reached for a fresh cigarette in her duffel bag sized purse on the passenger seat.

Jeff, my grandpa, was the one she always talked about when she was reminiscing about romance. I had a couple memories, but most of what I knew came from stories, illustrated by photo albums and silent home movies.

"Meemaw, how old are you?" I asked as she pulled the car into the school parking lot.

She flopped her arm across the top of the front seat. She crooked her neck and grinned at me. Her eyes were moist, which made them sparkle through her glasses.

"A lady never tells," she said, and winked.

She twisted further, trying to make eye contact with Aamilah.

"Be nice to my grandson, young lady. He's one of a kind."

"Yes ma'am," Aamilah replied.

My face burned and my throat tightened.

"Th-th-th-thanks for the r-r-r-ride," I said. I grabbed my backpack and jumped out of the back seat.

Aamilah joined me. We walked toward the long corrugated metal awning that covered the entry to the low brick school building. Across the top of the building, a faded wooden billboard proclaimed in chipped blue and yellow paint, *"Pinesburg Middle School – Home of the Mudcats – 1988 Region XII Basketball Champs"*.

"Been a l-l-l-long t-t-time since we won anyth-th-thing, huh?" I asked.

"It sure has," a Caribbean voice answered.

CHAPTER 21

Ms. Pendleton stood in the middle of the front doors, arms crossed and toe tapping on the worn mat.

"You can change that, Atlas," she continued. "Spelling bee practice today after school."

I hung my head.

"Spelling bee?" Aamilah asked.

"Yes. Atlas is brilliant and it's time for the world to see him shine." Ms. Pendleton opened the door.

"Can I ask where you two have been? Miss Turpentine tells me you left the bus, young lady – and you never showed up, young man."

"Yes ma'am, I did leave the bus. I was worried about Atlas." Aamilah replied.

We followed Ms. Pendleton into the building. The odor of moldy drywall coated with fresh paint was actually comforting. As crazy as the last month had been, getting back into the simple routine of school felt like slipping on my favorite shoes. The tread might be rubbed down and the broken shoelaces might be dirty and knotted at the eyelet, but they were mine.

She ushered us into her office and closed the door.

"Sit down."

As we plopped into the beanbags, I struggled to get comfortable.

I wish this beanbag would just swallow me whole.

I glanced at the clock on the wall.

8:05.

Though it felt like much longer, only thirty-five minutes had passed since I ran out of the house. Since I didn't help Wyatt.

"Is Wyatt h-h-here?" I asked.

"Yes, why do you ask, Atlas?" Ms. Pendleton asked. She leaned against the front of her desk. Her long legs, crossed at the ankles, ended between our beanbags.

"He wasn't on the bus." Aamilah answered.

"What about Bi...er, Har-Har-Harold?"

"Harold is suspended today. For your fight on the bus." Ms. Pendleton glared at me. "Are you still having trouble with him?"

"No ma'am. I m-m-mean, not reall-ll-lly. No. No tr-

tr-trouble." I twisted the thin pleather in my hands, rolling the tiny beads underneath around with my fingers.

Ms. Pendleton placed her hands on the front edge of her desk and leaned down.

"I have a feeling you're not being completely honest with me. You wouldn't try to feed me Johnny cakes without butter and honey, are you?"

There was no way I was going to tell her about Wyatt and the plot to trap Big Harold. I shrugged my shoulders.

"No ma'am."

She looked at Aamilah. "Do you know what's going on wit' 'dis boy 'ere?"

"What do you mean, Miss Pendleton?" Aamilah asked.

I looked over at Aamilah. Her bare brown arm ran along her side, ending in her lanky fingers tightly pressed into the bright blue beanbag. She dug her nails in as she awaited Ms. Pendleton's response.

"I mean," Ms. Pendleton stood and walked around to the far side of her desk. "I want to know what happened this morning. Why you," she pointed her long dark finger at Aamilah, "ran off the bus, and," she turned her hand and placed me in her crosshairs, "why you weren't on it at all. And how the two of you," she pointed at each of us with both hands, "came to be brought to school by Atlas's grandmother?"

She crossed her arms and tilted her head.

"That's what I mean," she added.

"Miss Pendleton, it's m-m-my f-f-fault. I ran into th-th-the woods be-be-because I saw something st-st-st-strange. The other kids told Aamilah and she was just b-b-b-being a good friend," I answered.

I sat as upright as I could and pulled my backpack into my lap.

"What was the strange thing you saw, Atlas?" she asked.

"It was like a r-r-r-red light in th-th-the sk-sky."

"A red light in the sky? Really?" Ms. Pendleton's brow and lip wrinkled as she questioned my veracity.

"Yes."

She shot Aamilah a quizzical stare.

Aamilah looked at me then back at Ms. Pendleton. She shrugged her shoulders and held her palms up.

"That's what he told me, too," she replied.

"You," Ms. Pendleton pointed at me. Her eyes were piercing. " She continued in her natural Carribean accent. "You gonna run me clean outa grace, young man." She smiled and relief washed over me.

"No more chances. No more nonsense. No more make believe," Ms. Pendleton said. She reached into her top drawer and pulled out a pad of pink paper.

"Here's your hall pass. Get to class."

Aamilah and I peeled out of the beanbags. I grabbed the pass and nearly ran out of the door.

I heard the unmistakable sound of Ms. Pendleton clearing her throat. I stopped just outside her office door.

"You're welcome, Atlas," she said.

"Oh, yes. Thank you, Miss Pendleton."

"You won't be riding the bus home either," she said. "Be in my office twenty minutes after school dismisses. We'll be going to room one seventeen for spelling bee practice. I'll call your mother to let her know."

I nodded. A knot tightened in my stomach. I walked out of her office without another word. It wasn't so difficult to get Miss Pendleton's forgiveness. Wyatt's, on the other hand...

CHAPTER 22

I slid my tray down and joined him at our usual lunch table, in the back corner of the cafeteria, under the upright speakers that were used for assemblies and the always awkward but faculty favorite, the junior high battle of the bands.

"Where were you?" Wyatt asked as he slammed his tray down on our table, shared as usual with no one.

I picked at an oozing sloppy joe with my plastic fork.

"The cr-cr-craziest th-thing happened, Wyatt. Th-th-the case opened this mor-morning – "

He cut me off. "The case? That we dug up? Whatever. Look at me, Atlas. Look at me."

I lifted my eyes from the lumpy rust colored meat

soup and looked at Wyatt. He had a square bandage on his neck and a lump on his forehead.

"I'm lucky I wasn't hurt worse. I don't care about that stupid case. I care – make that *cared* – about my friend. Friends show up for the biggest thing of the year. Friends show up for a fight. Friends don't bail because of some case. No matter how mysterious."

"Wyatt, you don't understand. The thing lit up my room. Then shocked me. Then this tiny fairy elf girl – I don't know what she is – appeared after I fell in the hole…"

"What are you talking about?" Wyatt leaned over his tray, knocking his milk carton over.

"Crap!" He exclaimed.

The cold creamy white dribble rolled across the table, like clouds gathering before a storm. Wyatt quickly straightened the carton and dabbed at the spill. Though he was focused on the mess, he continued to lecture me on friendship.

"Atlas, who else has got your back? Anyone? Who else has stuck with you since we were little? No one. That's who. No one but me."

"I know," I sputtered. I took a sip of juice to drown the building lump in my throat. It was no help. My eyes clouded with tears.

"I don't get it. You're always in a different world, in your imaginary places, your fantasyland. Now you're talking about fairies? Elves? Come on, Atlas. If I can't count on you, maybe I need to recount the reasons for our friendship."

He wadded up the milk-soaked napkins and slapped them on the corner of his tray. He leaned back and folded his arms.

"No. Wyatt," I replied. "How m-m-much time is l-l-left for lunch?" I asked as I looked to the clock at the far end of the cafeteria. "We've got fifteen minutes," I said. "Just come s-s-s-see the b-b-b-book in my locker."

I stood.

"And then what?" Wyatt asked. "Is the book going to help you keep your word? Is the book going to help you quit visiting fantasy worlds? Is the book going to help me trust you again?"

"I don't know." I hung my head. "But it might."

I stared at my tray. The creamed corn and sloppy joe looked even less appealing than when I'd sat down, if that was possible. The brownie looked like a dried mud brick.

"My appetite's gone anyway. Just give me f-f-five min-minutes, ok?" I pleaded.

"Fine," Wyatt huffed. He stood up and followed me down the hall to our lockers.

We stood at the row of rusting metal cabinets for a few seconds.

"What are you waiting for?" Wyatt asked.

"Nothing," I replied. "I'm ju-ju-ju-just nervous, is all."

I twisted the dial on my built in combination lock and pulled the door open. The thick spine of the book was buried under torn notebook paper, wedged between unread science books, right where I placed it after the morning meeting with Ms. Pendleton.

I looked up and down the empty hallway.

"Let's take it in th-there to read," I said as I pointed to the boys' bathroom next to the *Reduce – Reuse – Recycle* bulletin board.

"Fine," Wyatt answered. He walked away while I grabbed the book with both hands. I followed him into the bathroom. My hands began shaking as we walked through the door.

Wyatt leaned against the middle sink.

I looked around the room. Two cracked mirrors, an empty paper towel holder. Three stalls without doors, and three urinals. Dried toilet paper spit wads stuck to the ceiling. The janitor had left a couple empty boxes in the corner, between the trashcan and the single window in the room, a tiny chicken wire reinforced pane near the top of the wall.

"Over there," I said.

We walked across the shoe-scuffed linoleum toward the empty pile of boxes. I set the book atop it and looked at Wyatt.

"You ready?" I asked.

"For what?" He asked.

"I don't know, exactly. B-b-but, I th-think it's someth-th-thing that's out of this world."

CHAPTER 23

THIS HISTORY, ORIGINALLY RECORDED ON THE GREAT ONYX TABLETS, IS COPIED HEREIN AT THE COMMAND OF KING BARTHOLOMEW, OF THE HOUSE OF YUDARNA, EIGHTH KING OF CELESTERIA, HEIR TO THE THRONE OF THESTER, KING OF THE NECESSARY DREAM.

I whistled softly after I read the large print on the thin, delicate, nearly translucent first page. I licked my finger and peeled the corner of the page over.

THE WORKS OF PHILLION, CREATOR OF CELESTERIA AND ALL THAT REMAIN. THE BLESSING AND COMMAND OF THE IMMORTAL, ETERNAL ENDURING WORDS THAT GIFTED ALL APHARMARI AND THEIR WAYWARD BRETHREN, HEREAFTER NAMED AS ONE WITH THEIR GREAT DEFILER, THE REPHARIAMISI.

AFTER THE REPHARIAMISI REBELLION, PHILLION RETURNED TO THE FOREST OF THE GOBAH TREES, PLACE OF ORIGIN AND MANIFESTATION OF THE NECESSARY DREAM. HIS BESEECHING OF THE ANCIENT WOODLAND YIELDED A FINAL CREATION, HUMAN. SET AT LIBERTY AND OBSERVED FROM AFAR, THE HUMAN WAS GIVEN POWER AND INGENUITY YET BLINDED FROM THE ETERNAL REALM. HIS WORKS WILL EVENTUALLY BE KNOWN, AND HIS GLORY WILL BE FULL.

AND PHILLION APPOINTED THE FAITHFUL APHARMARI TO GUARD AND GUIDE THE DREAMS OF HUMAN PROGENY, FOR IN THEM ARE BIRTHED ALL THAT IS TO BE AND THROUGH THEM BOTH THE FIRST CREATION AND THE SECOND CREATION REFLECT THE MAJESTY OF PHILLION, THE NECESSARY DREAM.

"Can you believe this!?" I exclaimed.

I turned to Wyatt, who was watching as my finger traced the letters.

"Believe what? It's all gibberish. It just looks like the code on Crankenstein's garage," Wyatt said.

"Are you serious? You can't read it?" I nearly knocked the book to the floor. I tucked my thumb in the page and held it with both hands.

"Yes, I'm serious," he replied, "I mean, it's strange, kinda cool, but it's just the crazy symbols. It doesn't tell us anything."

"It doesn't? Then how come I can re-re-read it?" I looked at him closely. There was no blink to his eyes, no squirm to his stance, no tightening to his lips. He was telling the truth.

"The green fog!" I nearly shouted, remembering my encounter with Talia. "This isn't a fantasy, Wyatt. This is real."

"What's real?" A deep voice asked.

Wyatt and I both turned and looked at the bathroom entrance.

"Oh, hel-hel-hello Principal Wilk-Wilk-Wilkins," I said.

I dropped the book on the box behind me and shuffled in front of it to block his view.

"Real smooth," Wyatt muttered under his breath.

"What's that Wyatt?" Principal Wilkins approached.

"Nothing sir," Wyatt answered. He slid alongside me. "You wearing a new suit, Principal Wilkins?" He asked. "It looks really sharp."

His usual garb, a corduroy jacket with faux wood buttons, an oxford dress shirt with frayed collar and cuffs, was replaced by a navy blue business suit and red power tie.

"Cool p-p-p-pocket square," I added.

Principal Wilkins stepped back and turned to the mirror.

"You really think so?" He preened and primped his hair, tightened his necktie and looked back at us. His grin was reminiscent of a girl looking at her parents' for approval after trying on a prom dress. Like good parents, Wyatt and I sure weren't going to tell him the truth - that awkwardness never gets erased, no matter how fine the fabric.

"Looking real good, sir," Wyatt answered.

"Def-def-definite-t-t-def-definitely," I added.

"Well, we better get back to lunch so we can finish up before class. Don't want to be late, right Principal Wilkins?" Wyatt said.

"Very true," he replied and turned to the bank of urinals.

I wedged the book between my arm and side, away from Principal Wilkins sight, and we started to walk out of the bathroom.

"You boys keep up the good work, ok?" Principal Wilkins said as he flipped his tie over his shoulder and scooted up to urinal number two.

"For sure," Wyatt answered.

The hallway was filled with students. Clusters of cool kids, bunches of boisterous bedlam, and small circles of whispers; all jostled together in the main artery of the school. They were flooding in, tightly packed, preserved in their clique bubbles, finishing lunch and swapping homework answers before classes resumed.

The bell to finish lunch was soon to ring. I scrunched up against the wall, desperate to get to my locker and secure the book without any incident. If Big Harold hadn't been suspended, I probably would have hid in the bathroom until the halls were clear.

"That was cl-cl-close," I whispered to Wyatt.

"Sure. Atlas, I'm glad you got your book but I don't like pretending that it has real words in it. And I can't pretend that this morning didn't happen."

Wyatt's locker was a dozen spots ahead of mine. We reached his first. He opened it and continued talking as he grabbed his materials for the afternoon classes.

"I just can't keep up the charade. We're in middle school, Atlas. Soon, we'll be in high school. I can't play kid games forever. Maybe it's best if we just don't hang out right now."

He shut his locker and walked away, leaving nothing but a frigid wall of abandoned friendship between us.

Now what?

No Wyatt. No friends. No one.

"Should have been me instead of Charlie," I mumbled.

"Don't say that. Don't *ever* say that."

I looked up.

Aamilah. Her familiar doe eyes and raven hair peeked around the edges of her locker door. She smiled.

"You are alive for a reason, Atlas. Just because things don't make sense right now, doesn't mean there's not a purpose behind it. I don't know what to say except I do believe that God has a plan."

"Yeah, well, I'd li-li-like to know where G-G-God is r-r-r-right now."

"He is everywhere. He is always near."

"Sure, Aamilah, easy f-f-for y-y-y-you to say," I replied, "Be-be-because everyth-th-thing is easy for you to s-s-s-say, isn't it? You d-d-don't know what th-th-this is

158

like."

I slipped around her to open my locker, just three lockers away from where she stood. I held the book as tight as I could against my side with my right hand while trying to turn the combination tumbler with my left hand. It wasn't easy.

Aamilah slammed her locker door, which startled me. The book slipped down my side. I lurched to catch it and pinned it against my thigh with both hands.

"You're right Atlas," Aamilah said. "I don't know what it's like to be you. But, before you get all lost in self-pity, why don't you consider what it's like to be me? Ever cross your mind what it's like to come from another country – another world – and be surrounded by people who whisper about your family and call your dad a terrorist?"

Her eyes blazed and began to fill with tears.

I didn't know what to say. She was right.

"I'm sorry your brother died, I really am," she continued, tears now dripping through her long lashes onto her light blue shirt. "And I know you only have one friend, Wyatt. But at least you have *one* friend. Some of us don't have any."

She turned and raced through the hall, before I could respond.

The ringing bell summoned us back to class. All I wanted to do was crawl inside my locker and erase the last month of my life.

CHAPTER 24

I was rattled from my encounter with Aamilah. By the time Civics class started, the final class of the day, I could only think about going home. As Mr. Walters, who everyone calls The Walrus because of his extra chins and wire brush moustache, gesticulated about the importance of proper infrastructure in communities, all I could think about was my fractured friendships.

If only I'd shown up two minutes sooner, Wyatt would have been fine and Harold would have gotten his.

The elf fairy girl said nothing is accidental.
Nothing?
How could nothing be accidental?

What does that mean about Charlie?
Charlie's note!

Squished down in my pocket, bunched in by spare change and friction of the day's movements, rested a single scrap of paper that held the only encouragement I could find.

I pulled it out. The creases from repeated unfolding were wearing away at the ink.

I flattened it against my desk and indulged in yet another reading. Reading it was like finding the eye in a hurricane. It was like breathing fresh air after a week in a coalmine. It kept me alive.

Dear Atlas,

I ben itching to tell you some things lately. I know you have a lot of dreams. They are cool. I wished I was smart like you. I don't always appreshiate what you like. I don't always ~~understand~~ ~~figure out~~ ~~know how to say~~

Coach Jefferson said something last week and I can't hardly get it out my brains. He said we got to never change what we was made to be, no matter what other people think. I see you all

161

the time playing alone, lost in day dreaming
and I know you feel kinda diffrent.
I think you should be yourself. keep
dreaming, because nobody will ever

You should just be yourself. Charlie wrote that I should
do what I want, that I shouldn't worry about other people's
opinions.

*Were Charlie's words accidental? He never wrote me
anything my whole life.*

Did Charlie know what was going to happen?

No, that's not possible.

"What do you have there, Atlas?"

I jolted up in my seat and slapped my hands on the
note.

The Walrus was blowing over me, his lisp whistling
the last syllable in my name. I hadn't heard a sound, yet
suddenly he was beside my desk, puffy and disapproving.

"I said, what do you have there, Atlas?"

"Atlas Forman," the school intercom announced,
"Please report to Miss Pendleton's office immediately."

I slid the note off the desk, folded it in half twice and
stood up. I bumped the Walrus's large belly with my elbow
as I rose.

"Sorry, Mr. W-W-W-Walters. B-B-But I have to get
to th-th-the office. Right?"

I squeezed past him into the aisle.

He grunted and glared at me.

"Turn to the chart on page three forty one," he announced to the class. "Make sure you get your assignment done, Mr. Forman," he said as he waddled back to his perch behind the lectern at the front of the room.

CHAPTER 25

The empty hall echoed with the tinny clink of the second hand on the giant clock near the main entrance. In five minutes, the place would be buzzing with escaping students, another day X'ed out of the calendar. Another day closer to summer, another day closer to freedom.

I gathered my stuff from my locker and filled my backpack with notebooks and workbooks, and then, *the book*. I dropped my backpack to the floor between my feet as I held the mysterious book. I thumbed through the opening pages until my eyes landed on a particularly worn page. The book naturally fell open, as though this section had been read often.

HUMAN, AS THE RENALL BENJI OF THE APHARMARI, WITH RARE EXCEPTION, DO NOT CONTEMPLATE THEIR FATE WITH URGENCY UNTIL TIME IS NEARLY EXTINGUISHED. THE NOBLE AND MOST HIGH CALLING FOR EACH APHARMARI IS TO PROTECT THE INNOCENCE AND SHIELD THE VIRTUE OF THEIR RENALL BENJI; OF PHILLION'S MOST BELOVED: HUMAN.

THEIR BATTLES ARE NOT WITH EACH OTHER, THOUGH THEY BELIEVE IT TO BE SO. THEIR WARS ARE NOT OVER LAND, POWER, CULTURE, OR CREED. THEY LONG FOR PEACE, YET IT REMAINS UNFOUND. IT IS THROUGH DEFILEMENT BY THE REPHARIAMISI, WHOSE ETERNAL REBELLION IS AN ALL-CONSUMING FIRE; HUMAN BECOMES TWISTED, PERVERTED AND MAIMED. IT IS ONLY THROUGH THE ALLEGIANCE AND FORTITUDE OF THE APHARMARI THAT HUMAN AND THE ENTIRE

EARTH IS NOT UTTERLY DESTROYED.

THE PARAMOUNT WORK THEN, IS FOR ALL APHARMARI TO SET ASIDE PERSONAL DESIRES, ALL INDIVIDUAL AMBITION, AND SERVE. SERVE HUMAN. SHIELD HUMAN. SAVE HUMAN. IN SO DOING, THE APHARMARI FULFILL AND RESTORE THE NECESSARY DREAM. ONE DAY, PHILLION WILL RETURN AND THE REPHARIAMISI WILL BE CAST INTO AN ENDLESS SPIRIT SLEEP. PILY WILL BE SEEN IN ALL HER GLORY, AND THE GOBAH TREES WILL SING FOR THE UNIVERSE TO HEAR. THE FAITHFUL APHARMARI WILL LIFT THEIR EYES AND SEE IT COME TO PASS.

THE BEGINNING OF THESE SIGNS WILL BE REVEALED AT THE COMING OF THE EKYLLION. HE IS NOT OF THE APHARMARI AND HE IS NOT OF CELESTERIA. HE IS HUMAN. BY HIS SPEECH HE SHALL

BE REVEALED. WITH TREMBLING LIPS AND STAMMERING TONGUE HE SHALL PROCLAIM VICTORY; AND THE APHARMARI WILL HEAR AND KNOW THE END OF SUFFERING HAS BEGUN.

Ekyllion.

That's what she called me.

The bell rang. A violent eruption of slamming doors and thudding feet ricocheted through the hall. I slammed the book shut and pushed it down into my backpack. A quick zip and I sprinted a few yards down the hall to Miss Pendleton's office.

"What took you so long?" she asked as I entered the outer office. She was leaning against the back wall, just outside her office door. The pearls that usually draped her neck were absent. Her eyes were storm clouds. This was our third meeting in just a couple weeks in which her greeting was a grimace.

"I'm sor-sor-sorry," I said. "I was ju-ju-just g-g-g-getting my stuff." I held up my backpack.

"Come in my office."

She turned and walked in without waiting.

I hurried in behind her. As I walked into the office, I sensed the presence of another person. Sitting in a chair, on the far side of the two beanbags, was Marjorie Jenkins, the mocking red devil.

She stared at me. Her eyes were firm and stern, like she was prepared to negotiate a corporate takeover. Uneasiness crept – no, swept – over me.

"I got a call just after lunch that Harold Randolph is in the hospital. He has fractured ribs, internal bleeding and a broken jaw," Miss Pendleton said. She sat behind her desk. I stood just inside the door. She didn't motion for me to sit.

"What? Wh-Wh-Who?" I asked.

"Harold Randolph," she repeated. "Your classmate."

My puzzled expression obviously frustrated her. She sighed and doubled over, resting her head on the desk.

I looked over at Marjorie, my eyes wide, eyebrows arched.

"Big Harold," Marjorie whispered.

"B-B-B-Big Har-Har-Harold," I repeated.

Miss Pendleton sat up. "Yes, Big Harold. He has a full name. His given name. Harold Randolph."

Miss Pendleton stood up. She braced her hands against the credenza behind her desk and briefly stared at the ceiling.

"I have spoken to the bus driver and some of the students, including Marjorie," Miss Pendleton nodded in the red devil's direction, "and it seems like you were one of the last people to see him today. As you know, he was suspended," she paused.

"Yes – "

"For fighting," she interrupted me. "*With you.* Since you have a – ahem – history with Harold, I naturally wanted to speak with you. Marjorie tells me you and Harold got into a hullabaloo this morning. She said you were the last person with him. Is this true?"

My eyes flit a glare at Marjorie. I stiffened and blinked, then looked at Miss Pendleton, whose gaze remained fixed on me.

Relax, I thought.

"I did see him but th-that was be-be-before school."

"Marjorie told me that Harold threw you down and then tossed you into a hole in the ground?" Miss Pendleton's interrogation intensified.

"Yes. B-B-But when I came to, he was gone."

"Came to?"

"Yes. I think I b-b-blacked out f-f-for a second."

"And you didn't try to find him? You didn't go after him?"

"Miss P-P-Pen-Pendleton," I answered. "I did not. Even if I would have, I couldn't hurt h-h-him. He-He-He's twice my size!"

"Atlas," Miss Pendleton said. She leaned over her desk. Her demeanor softened. A grin slowly formed.

"I wasn't accusing you of hurting him. I know you wouldn't do anything that savage. But, I hoped maybe you saw where he went. Harold told the police that he was jumped from behind and he doesn't know who attacked him. I told them I'd find out if any of our students saw anything. Which brings us to this moment. To this meeting."

Miss Pendleton sat down.

"Marjorie, you can go. Thank you."

Marjorie slipped out of her chair and walked toward me. As she passed by, a smirk danced across her freckled face.

Miss Pendleton saw me roll my eyes at the ginger-haired snitch.

"Atlas, be respectful," she admonished. "Now, sit down."

I slid down the wall, and knelt on the beanbag before rolling onto my butt. I crossed my legs and leaned back to rest my head against the cool cinder block wall.

"Now, just to be sure, is there anything else that you want to tell me about Harold? I talked to Wyatt, and…"

"Wyatt?" I interrupted.

"Yes. He said that he was in the altercation this morning but he ran to his house and didn't see where Harold went. Wyatt said that the two of you were planning on," she made air quotes with her slim fingers, "getting Harold back for what he'd done to you. Is that true? Were you plotting to injure Harold?"

"Yes," I replied. "We did tr-tr-try to get him b-b-back. But it b-b-backfired. It w-w-was my fault."

"What was your fault?"

I didn't want to tell her about digging the pit or getting delayed by the case and the red light and...but what should I tell her? More importantly, what did Wyatt tell her? If our stories didn't match things would only get worse.

"Atlas?" She pressed.

"Uh, it w-w-was my fault. I mean my idea."

"That's interesting. Wyatt said it was his idea."

"Well, uh, it was a j-j-j-joint ef-ef-effort." I clutched the beanbag and rocked forward.

"I see. Well, I have to say you and Wyatt are good friends. You both took the blame. That's unusual. Even for grown-ups."

She stared at her gleaming wooden desktop, "Actually, especially for grown-ups. Now, one last time, is there anything else you want to tell me about this morning and Harold?"

There were lots of things I could have told her. And some things I really wanted to tell her. She would believe me. Even about the book. She was always in my corner.

Should I show her the book?

"Nope. Th-Th-That's pretty mu-mu-much it," I finally answered.

"Ok. Well, I certainly hope the police find whoever hurt Harold." Miss Pendleton turned her back to me. She rummaged through a stack of files on the credenza and whispered to herself.

171

"He's going to miss more school because of this. He can't get any more behind in his work. It's the last thing he needs; after all he's been through - his parent's divorce, his sister's cancer. Poor Harold." She turned around and flopped several binders on her desk.

"Now, Mr. Forman. It's time for spelling bee practice."

CHAPTER 26

Miss Pendleton led me down the hall to the next challenge. Apparently, today was destined to be a never-ending gauntlet of horrible experiences. Physical, psychological, supernatural, emotional; was there any remaining area of existence that hadn't been tested?

As we walked into Room One Seventeen, I answered my own question. There was an area that had yet to be tested. Family.

A long plastic table was centered near the front of the room. Between the table and the chalkboard was a small wooden podium. Four rust-tinged metal folding chairs were arranged in a perfect row, like a firing squad.

Seated in the closest chair, with one arm around

Coach Jefferson and one arm waving at me was my dad, wearing his navy suit and plea bargain smile.

"H-H-H-Hey D-D-Dad, uh, what are y-y-you doing here?"

"Mom called me," Dad stood up, "she had one of those meetings of hers. I left court to come over here and get you."

Coach Jefferson tugged on his visor and growled, "Hello Atlas, good to see you son." He didn't stand.

"Hello s-s-sir."

"Miss Pendleton, thank you for trying to help Atlas," Dad said. He glanced at his wristwatch, hidden behind cuff-link clasped cuffs. "How long do you think this will be?"

I looked at Miss Pendleton. Her smile flickered but held.

"Thank you for coming, Mister Forman. The practice will take thirty to forty-five minutes."

"Atlas, I know you're nervous," she said, "but, we're for you. Coach Jefferson volunteered to be part of the spelling bee prep team. And your dad left work to come. So, what do you say? You've got a good head. Turn round fast, eh?"

"Yes ma'am." I slouched to the front of the room as Miss Pendleton sat next to Coach Jefferson. She distributed a couple sheets of paper to Dad and Coach.

"Ok, Atlas," she began, "first, why don't you put your backpack down?"

"I'll hold it for you, son," Dad said. He walked around the table and stood near me.

"It's ok, Dad," I said. "I'll just set it d-d-down here." I slipped it off my shoulders and laid it behind my feet as I stepped to the podium.

Dad reached down for the backpack but I scooted back to block his reach. He paused, bent over, and looked up at me.

"What's the problem, Atlas?" He asked. As he stood, he blew a puff of air out of the corner of his mouth to push his always immaculate hair back into place.

"Nothing. I just want to keep my bag cl-cl-close, that's all."

He stepped back.

"Fine, whatever," he replied and walked away.

After Dad was seated, Miss Pendleton began.

"Atlas, I know –," she looked down the table at Coach and Dad, "we know – that this isn't easy. And you've never done this before. But, you know as well as I do you're the best speller in this school. Maybe the best this school has ever had."

Dad puffed up a little in his chair.

Coach pushed his chair back and folded his arms across his cannonball stomach.

"So, here's the deal. We will practice this week, and then you'll be in a simulated spelling bee with a few of your classmates. In three weeks, the county spelling bee will take place. Win that, and you're off to regionals on July fourth weekend."

I stared at the caramel colored lectern before me. The black vinyl trim was peeling away from the cheap pressboard. I pressed against it and tried to slide the loose piece into the slot from which it had long since been released.

"Are you listening, Atlas?" Dad asked.

I looked up. "Yes."

"Well, act like it. Geez, Atlas, Miss Pendleton's giving you a chance here. A shot at doing something important, you know?"

"Mr. Forman," Miss Pendleton said.

He looked at her.

"Yes?" He asked.

"I think Atlas is under enough pressure already, don't you?"

"But, he has to…" he replied.

She cut him off.

"Let's just try before we make a judgment, ok?"

Dad joined Coach Jefferson in the folded arm pose as Miss Pendleton took full command of the session. I grinned, briefly.

"Atlas," she said. "The rules are as follows:

One, I will say the word to be spelled. I suggest you repeat the word out loud to be sure you've heard it right. Two, you may ask me to repeat it, or use it in a sentence.

You may also ask me to define the word. Third, and most important, you will be able to re-start spelling a word, but you can't change the order of the letters you already said. Does that make sense?"

"I th-think so," I replied. I looked at her over the goose necked microphone holder.

"Ok. Let's begin."

"Just a second, Miss P," Coach Jefferson sat up straight and put his fists on the table. "Gotta give this boy a little pep talk, alright?"

She waved her hand, granting permission.

"Allrighty then. Atlas, I don't know ya too well. But I knew your brother, Charlie. Kid was tougher than the crust on week-old bread. Loyal too. If he was with you, he was with you all the way. Now, I want you to dig down and show 'em what you're made of. Don't do this for me, or Miss P, or heck, even your daddy. Don't even do it for yourself, though Lord knows you need to. No, I'm telling you, do it for the one person who lost his chance to do something, anything, for the rest of the world. Do it for Charlie."

As he finished his speech, part of me was annoyed. Part of me was a little bit inspired. The biggest part of me was petrified. Adults say and do the most asinine things. Usually, it's best for kids to just go along with it. So I did.

"Yes, coach."

"Ok," Miss Pendleton sat up tall in her seat. "Let's begin. Atlas, you'll have two minutes per word. I'll use my watch as a timer, ok?"

I nodded.

"Are you ready, Atlas?" Miss Pendleton asked.

I nodded.

"Ok. Let's see what you've got."

CHAPTER 27

"Let's start with an easy one. Atlas, the first word is *PARALYZE. Par-a-lyze.*"

I froze. *How appropriate.*

"Do you need it used in a sentence?" Coach Jefferson offered.

I shook my head in response. I tightened my lips and gripped the sides of the podium. I closed my eyes.

"Para-Para-Para-lyze," I repeated.

"Paralyze," Miss Pendleton echoed.

"P-A-R-A-" I began. I could feel the letter "L" twisting my tongue. It danced in my head, taunting me. I squeezed my eyes tighter.

"L-Y-Z-E," I exhaled.

"Well, I'll be…" Dad whispered.

"Lookie there Preston! He's gonna do allright!" Coach Jefferson slapped Dad on the back.

"One word does not a champion make," Miss Pendleton counseled. My cheerleading section promptly calmed down.

"Right, of course," Coach Jefferson said. "But, it's a good start, Miss P. Now, Atlas, just drive it home son. Slow and steady. You can't score two touchdowns in one play. Grind it out. Three yards and a cloud of dust. Take it to 'em."

I didn't know what I was supposed to "take to 'em," but I assumed he was speaking metaphorically. There was nothing to take and no 'em to take it to.

"Next word," Miss Pendleton announced. "TRAVESTY. Tra-ve-sty. Meaning, disguised so as to be ridiculous. A grotesque imitation of a classic work, Tra-ve-sty."

Another appropriate word for the moment. If Miss Pendleton was shooting for irony, she was hitting bulls-eyes. If this wasn't a grotesque imitation of classic work, nothing was. A stutterer enters a spelling bee as some kind of quasi-speech therapy.

"Tr-tr-travesty," I repeated.

Dad's chair suddenly screeched, startling all of us.

"Sorry," he whispered. He shuffled it closer to the table and leaned forward.

180

"Travesty," he repeated.

"That Mueller game last season was a travesty. Boys played like a constipated elephant. Fat and slow," Coach added.

"Coach Jefferson," Miss Pendleton said. "We are not here to re-hash your football games." She pointed to me. "We are here to help Atlas win a spelling bee."

"W-W-W-Win?" I asked.

"Yes, Atlas. Win," she answered. "I've started the timer. The word is travesty."

"Traves-s-sty," I said.

"T-R," I began.

"A-V," I bit my lip.

T-R-A-V, I thought.

"E-S-T-Y," I finished. I sighed. Then, something unexpected happened. I smiled.

I looked at the three of them. Polished, pristine Dad. Plump, positive Coach Jefferson. Prescient, poised Miss Pendleton. Another Marty-ism entered my head:

"Makes about as much sense as a tuxedo on a hobo."

Like a tuxedo on a hobo.

That's how I felt when we started. After I spelled two more words correctly, I at least felt like I deserved to wear a collared shirt. I stumbled on a few words, then bounced back to get five in a row correct.

"Last word, Atlas," Miss Pendleton said after we'd been going at it for over half an hour. "You're twenty for twenty-seven so far. A good start."

"Yes, a great start," Dad said, his face no longer sour. For the first time since I was a child, he looked genuinely proud of me.

"Ok, Atlas, final word," Miss Pendleton said. The three of them leaned forward at the same time. Six eyes filled with hope, stared at me.

"Finish strong. Fourth quarter," Coach Jefferson whispered. I looked down at him. He and Dad had their arms locked, like a couple eager benchwarmers with the game on the line.

"PHANTASMA. *Fan-taz-ma*. An illusion, a vision, a dream. Also, an apparition or ghost, PHANTASMA."

"Phantasma," I whispered. "Hmmm. What is the l-l-language of or-origin?"

"French. Here's a sentence," Miss Pendleton answered. "The boy wasn't sure if the luminescent figure was real or if his mind had imagined the phantasma."

That's close to home, I thought. I closed my eyes again. *Nothing is accidental*, the elf fairy girl had said.

Talia, I thought. That was her name. I saw her again, floating before me. She was breathtaking, dainty yet bold. No pretense. No pretending.

"Atlas, At last, Atlas," I heard in my mind's ear. She said I was the one.

Ekyllion. She had said that word. It was in the book. I clenched my teeth. Was she a phantasma?

182

"Atlas."

"Atlas," Miss Pendleton called, "time is ticking. The word is Phantasma."

"P-H-A-A-A," I stumbled.

"P-H-A," I began anew.

"Sorry. Let me st-st-start over," I said.

"P-H-A," I opened my eyes.

"N-T-A," I lifted my chin.

"S-M-A." I smiled.

"Got it!" Dad yelled.

"Is that right?" Coach Jefferson asked.

"I'm sorry Atlas. The multiple a's when you first started would be counted as separate. That word would be misspelled," Miss Pendleton said.

"That's not fair," Dad banged the table.

"The good news is," Miss Pendleton stood up. "You spelled the word right. You spelled all the words right. You just need to control the repeated letters. If you can find a way to stop yourself when you feel..."

"When I f-f-feel? All I do-do-do is feel. Feel the j-j-jokes. Feel the insults. F-F-F-Fee-Feel the rejection. Do you know how-how-how hard th-th-this is?" I asked. My face burned with shame. I grabbed my backpack. "I tried, Miss P-P-Pendleton."

"Atlas, I know. Please don't lose heart," she walked around the table and stood facing me. Her dark eyes were vibrant, pushing me and pulling me in at the same time. "You were not born for average, Atlas. You were not named among the ordinary. You are a dreamer. Dreams are conceived at night, in the dark, when no one sees. They are born in the heat of hard work, in the midday sun. I will work with you, for my dream is for your dreams to come true."

"Yes, M-M-Miss Pendleton. I know." I slipped my right arm through the shoulder strap of my backpack.

"Good game, son," Coach Jefferson said. He walked up and tousled my hair. "Get a good night's sleep and we'll go after 'em tomorrow."

'Em. Who are 'em? Why are we getting 'em?

"Y-Y-Yes S-S-Sir."

"Allright, Atlas, let's go," Dad walked toward the door. "Thank you, Miss Pendleton. Atlas will be ready to go tomorrow. Meredith will pick him up."

"Thank you, Mr. Forman," Miss Pendleton answered.

"Looks like another Forman boy rises to the occasion, huh Preston," Coach Jefferson said.

"Looks like it." Dad thumped his chest. "Forman men got what it takes."

I followed Dad into the hall.

He put his arm around my shoulder and jostled me back and forth.

"Way to go, Atlas. You sure did me proud in there." He continued pushing me back and forth aggressively as we walked past the row of lockers and out to the parking lot.

"Why so quiet?" He asked as we reached his car.

"You dr-dr-drove the Cor-Cor-Corvette?" I asked.

"Yes. It's a beautiful day. In more ways than one." He held his arms aloft, and stared up at the bright blue sky.

"Ok, let's go home. What do you want for dinner? Pizza? Burgers? You name it, it's yours."

"Anything is f-f-fine with me," I replied.

"Well, you've got a few minutes to think about it. I have to swing by the office before we go home. Hop in, let's go."

I opened the low-slung heavy door and slid into the front seat. The supple red leather hugged my hips. The wood inlaid glove compartment practically glowed. Dad didn't realize I'd never ridden in it before. He waxed this car like it was a religious ceremony. Even though I wasn't thrilled about the spelling bee, and there was plenty of unsettled stuff between us, for the moment I allowed myself to enjoy the ride.

After a whiplash-inducing take off from a red light, followed by the blistering rush of adrenaline as we sped through hilly curves, I now understood the reverence. I was ready to worship. The Church of Preston Forman's Corvette had a new convert.

CHAPTER 28

"Sit tight, Atlas," Dad said as he pulled into the parking space stenciled *C. Preston Forman, Esq.* "I just need to grab a few files and I'll be right back."

"Ok."

As Dad slammed the door, I cranked open the triangular window wedged between the windshield and the passenger door. I closed one eye and stared through the opening I'd just created. A few spots away, a large grassy area was dotted with picnic benches. A circular sidewalk surrounded the benches, anchored by a concrete water fountain.

As I thought about getting out to walk around the mini-park, a large vehicle pulled into the spot beside ours.

My view now obstructed, I looked over. A vintage station wagon stopped. The front end shuddered as the driver turned off the old engine.

I know that car, I thought.

I looked at the driver, who was sliding the large handle along the steering column into "park". Thick glasses. Pale skin. Neck beard.

Neck beard, I thought.

Dr. Crankenstein.

I slid down in my seat. I turned into a human accordion, head down, knees to my chest, hands and feet tucked away from view.

The stitching on my pant inseam made me think of train tracks.

It would be nice to jump on a train right about now.

Never been on a train before.

Never really wanted to.

They always look dirty, even the passenger cars.

A loud rap on the window brought my train contemplations to an instant halt.

I kept my head down.

Louder and harder, the noise of fist against window pushed me further into a scrunched up ball of arms and legs. I tried to look out the corner of my eye but my head was too low to see anything but the glistening upholstery on the armrest built into the doorframe.

The pounding resumed. It was joined by a voice calling my name.

"Atlas, Atlas. Come on, Atlas, open the door."

It didn't sound like Dr. Crankenstein. I slowly turned my head and looked out the driver's window.

"Open the door. Come on, son," Dad pleaded. He pointed to the ignition switch. Sure enough, his yellow and blue enamel "PHS Class of '84" key fob was swaying from the jolt of knocking on the window.

I sat up straight and looked out my window. The wood-paneled station wagon was gone. Dr. Crankenstein was gone.

"How long were you in there?" I asked my dad as I leaned over to unlock his door. He pulled the door open and answered my question.

"Just a minute. Like I said. Marci had the files ready for me. I just grabbed them off my desk and came straight back."

Dad slid into the driver's seat. He turned the key and the old 327 V-8 roared to life.

"What were you doing?" He asked.

"Nothing much."

"You were all twisted up like a pretzel. It looked like you were trying to make yourself invisible. Or do you always squish yourself into the smallest space possible when you're waiting in the car?"

Dad pressed the clutch and shifted into reverse. He

threw his arm around the back of my seat and craned his neck to see out the back window.

As he moved the car into position to exit the parking lot, he paused before shifting into first and looked at me.

"So, are you going to tell me why you were folded in half?" He asked.

"Oh, you know D-D-Dad. J-J-Just doing my silly imagination st-st-stuff."

"You sure?"

"Yes, I'm sure."

We drove out into the street. Dad turned left and turned up the radio.

"Oh, this is a good song. On days like this, I wish ol' Sabrina was a convertible. He patted the dash and smiled as he sang along:

> *Little red corvette*
> *Honey you got to slow down*
> *You're gonna run your little red Corvette*
> *Right in the ground,*
> *Right down to the ground*

"Sabrina?" I asked, starting to laugh.

Dad laughed. "Yes, that's what I call her. Named her after an old crush from Charlie's Angels…"

He suddenly turned the radio down.

"Charlie's angels," he said as we braked behind a row of cars at the main intersection in downtown Pinesburg. The stoplight was as red as the glow I'd seen in the sky over the past few weeks.

He glanced at me and whispered, "Charlie's angel. Atlas, do you think there's such a thing as angels?"

"I d-d-don't know, Dad," I replied.

"Well, if there are such a thing, they did a piss poor job protecting Charlie." He punched the dash.

"I g-g-guess – " I started to say.

"I mean, he was only seventeen years old," Dad said loudly. "He was a good kid."

Dad looked up. "What the heck? Angels? Charlie must not have had any."

"Or maybe – "

"Maybe nothing," Dad yelled. "He's gone and he shouldn't be. My son. My boy…"

He buried his head in the crook of his elbow. The sound of his sobs filled the car.

"I know, Dad," I began.

A horn behind us blared.

Dad lifted his head and glared in the rear view mirror.

"Freakin' jerk! I'm going, I'm going."

He stomped on the gas. The tires squealed and the back end shimmied as we left the horn-honker fading in the distance.

"Like they have a clue what it's like to lose a child."

CHAPTER 29

"We're home," Dad announced as we entered the kitchen from the garage.

Meemaw looked up from the sink, peeler in hand. A pail of unpeeled potatoes was set before her.

"Where were you boys?" She asked, continuing to work, spraying finger long strips of brown skin into the plastic kitchen trashcan.

"Well, Meemaw," Dad replied as he dropped his stack of files onto the table. "Atlas here is competing in a spelling bee."

Meemaw dropped the potato and the peeler.

"Say what?" She asked.

"You heard me," Dad answered. "Unless you forgot

your hearing aids again." He laughed.

"I don't wear hearing aids and you know it, Clarence." Meemaw used Dad's real first name whenever she wanted to get under his skin. Like duct tape, it always did the trick.

"Whatever, Rosemary," he replied.

"Snappy comeback, Clarence. What'd ya do? Use all your clever words up in the courtroom today?" Meemaw snorted.

"Nope," Dad answered. "Here's one - what's the difference between you and the tree stump out back?"

"I don't know, what?" Meemaw asked, hands on her hips.

"The tree stump doesn't try to pretend it has a brain." Dad chuckled and looked at me.

I shrugged my shoulders.

"Yeah, that went over about as good as a pregnant pole-vaulter," Meemaw replied. "You know, for a big time lawyer, you should have better material."

The telephone between the refrigerator and the toaster rang.

"Don't answer –" Dad began.

"Hello, Forman residence," Meemaw yapped into the receiver.

"That," Dad finished.

"Just a sec – you needing to holler at Preston?" Meemaw said. "Ok, let me grab him for you."

She held the phone out to Dad. He made a cutting

motion with his hand across his throat. He pointed outside and mouthed, *I'm not here.*

She didn't budge. She smiled and yelled, "Clarence, come get the phone!"

"Fine," Dad fumed. He snatched it from her hand.

"Hello, Preston Forman here," he said.

"As fun as th-th-this is, I'm going up to my room to get caught up on my work, ok?" I said.

"Hang on a sec, Atlas," Dad said, holding up his hand to me. He continued talking on the phone, "No, not you Jim. Hold on."

He covered the mouthpiece with his hand. "Just a minute Atlas, ok? Wait a sec, please?" He nodded toward Meemaw. "Help your grandmother peel the potatoes."

I set my backpack against the wall and walked over to Meemaw as Dad went back to his call. As we stripped the tubers of their skin, we overheard Dad's conversation. I wasn't paying close attention until I heard him say a familiar name.

"Harold Randolph?" Dad asked. "He goes to school with Atlas?"

I looked up from the potatoes instantly and stared at the back of Dad's head. Meemaw nudged me but I ignored her.

"His uncle? Going to be charged?" Dad spoke quickly.

"When's the hearing?" Dad looked at his wristwatch. "I don't think I can make it."

He listened for a minute or so.

"I already did my pro bono work this year, Jim. I'm not looking for more charity services. I know, I know. Besides, beating a kid? Come on, you know I can't take a case like that, even if he's innocent. I can't be seen next to someone getting accused of attacking a kid - attacking his own nephew. I could see the ads in the Mayor's race now. Forman doesn't care about the children, in fact, he defends child abusers –"

The voice on the other end interrupted.

"Yes, I said Mayor. You know I want to run –"

The voice on the other end interrupted again.

"So the guy has money? No, I just can't do it. Why don't you call Frank Beningham? He's a serviceable attorney, and he could probably use the big retainer this case is sure to bring. Truth be told, I could use the retainer, but no, I can't take this case."

Dad listened for a few seconds.

"Allright, Jim, I'll sleep on it. I'll give you my decision in the morning. Goodbye."

Dad handed the phone back to Meemaw and glared at her. "Couldn't let the machine get it, huh?"

"The machine?" she repeated. "I don't get you kids and your machines. Computers do everything. Gonna have computers pooping for you in a few years, I suppose."

"Atlas," Dad ignored Meemaw's weird and gross comment, "Do you know Harold Randolph?"

"Yes." I replied.

"Do you know anything about his family?"

"No, I don't"

"Did you know he was over at Eastern Regional Hospital? He got hurt pretty bad. He got beat up."

Dad stepped closer to me. "The cops arrested his uncle for aggravated battery, public intoxication and resisting arrest. Jim Dristen wants me to defend him. Seems Jim owes him one. How well do you know Harold?"

"I d-d-don't re-re-really. He's kind of a b-b-bully. But, I'm s-s-s-s-sorry he got hurt." I reached for my backpack.

"Allright, well, if you think there's anything I need to know, you'll tell me, right?"

"Sure, Dad. Can I go up to my r-r-r-room now?"

"Yeah, go ahead," Dad replied.

I flipped my bag to my left shoulder and walked out of the kitchen.

"Hey, one more thing," Dad called out.

I turned in the hallway and looked back through the narrow entrance to the kitchen. Meemaw was back to peeling, and Dad was peeling across the linoleum to reach me.

"You forgot to tell me what you wanted for dinner," he said as he stepped onto the faded blue runner centered on the hallway floor.

"Oh, it's ok, Dad. Whatever is fine with me."

I turned to keep walking.

195

"No. What do you want? Seriously, you name it."

He wasn't going to let me go without an answer. I leaned against the coat closet door, a few feet away from him.

"Uh, how about pizza?" I asked.

"Sounds good. You want the usual? Italian sausage, onions and mushrooms?" Dad was smiling bigger than I'd seen in a long time. I couldn't tell him that sausage, onions and mushrooms wasn't my usual pizza. It was Charlie's. I held my tongue; especially after the mention of the TV show in the car nearly undid him.

"Yes. You guessed it." I shot him a weak smile and turned toward the base of the stairs.

"How can ya'll eat that stuff?" Meemaw hollered. Guess she had put her hearing aids in, after all.

"We just can," Dad replied. "Everyone eats differently, Meemaw."

I stepped onto the creaking step and grabbed the loose banister. Its familiar wobble reminded me of Charlie. He was always sliding down it and getting yelled at. He must have crashed Mom's giraffe-motif umbrella stand once a week.

I was three steps into the climb when I heard Dad call my name again.

"Atlas?"

"Yes?" I answered, pausing to look over the stair railing.

"I just wanted to tell you to have fun up there. Don't be like me. You don't have to grow up all in one day."

I nodded and started climbing the stairs.

"Atlas?"

"Yes, Dad?" I replied, stopping once more.

"I love you."

"You too," I said. The lump in my throat pushed me up the steps before I could say any more.

I climbed to the top as quick as I could.

"Guess we do all grieve differently," I whispered as I turned down the hallway and entered my room.

CHAPTER 30

I shut the door and locked it. I dropped my backpack on my bed and dove to the floor and lifted my bedcover up. The case was still there, under the bed, flat open, just as I'd left it.

A flurry of dust swirled up as I grabbed the case, causing me to sneeze as I dragged it out.

Hard to believe less than twelve hours ago, this thing was singing and radiating, and shocking me.

I stood and lifted the case, still open, onto my bed. The soft gray lining reminded me of the fancy silverware drawer in Meemaw's china cabinet, though none of the forks or spoons ever gave me an electric shock.

The large stone was bursting with color. Without

the red glow, the music or the singing, it didn't seem very mysterious. It just looked like a pretty rock. I reached out my hand, just inches away from the rock for at least a minute, maybe longer. I inched my fingers closer and closer until a hair's breadth was all that separated us.

My shoulder started burning. My arm started tingling.

For some reason I looked around the room, like I was making sure no one was watching. I looked back at the sparkling purplish-gray beauty.

"The fish ain't never gonna just jump in your bucket," Marty's voice whispered in my head so clear and firm, it was like he was standing beside me.

I smiled. *You're right, Marty.*

That was all it took. I forced my hand into contact with the shiny stone. My flesh pressed in then recoiled. Not from shock. From temperature. The stone was freezing cold.

I rubbed it with both hands. The outer ring was smoother than the worn railing coming up the stairs. I pressed my fingers into the little nooks and crannies peppered throughout the stone's center. Tiny pinpricks nipped at my fingers. The inside of each small divot was ringed with miniature stalactites. Or stalagmites, I guess it didn't matter since the rock was sideways.

I spread my hands wide around the edge of the stone. A space just a fingernail width between the rock and the case lining, it was impossible to slip my hands under the rock and pull it out.

"There's more than one way to get coal out of the ground," I said, echoing the local old timers down at the barbershop. I slid my hands under the case and flipped it over on my bed.

I lifted the case and shook it like I was sifting a pan of dirt for gold. The stone remained ensconced.

I banged on the outside of the case with both fists, pounding on it and lifting it up, expecting the stone to fall onto the empty bed. My bed remained empty. I held the case above my head. The stone remained fixed inside. I shook it for a moment, and then remembered it was suspended over my head and would really hurt if it fell out onto my face. I set the case back on the bed, face down, and looked around my room for a tool.

The first thing to catch my eye was the ebony bookcase that had come in a box. Dad and I (mostly Dad) put it together a few years ago. It still looked like a do-it-yourself project, complete with leftover screws and uneven legs. Its three thick shelves held a smattering of books, toy soldiers and one very special picture, a picture I hadn't looked at it in forever.

It was a picture from our fishing trip with Marty when I was like seven or eight years old. Charlie's smile was big and bright as he held a tiny trout above my head. My missing front teeth grin was pure delight. Marty was in the background, draped in yellow rain gear, his beard speckled with bait bits.

It was framed in burnt orange synthetic leather, with cream-colored stitching around the border. I grabbed it and traced the stitching with my finger.

I closed my eyes and remembered that day - bouncing for hours in Marty's worn-out Jeep. The pit stop for greasy burger and all-I-could-eat French fries. Charlie's lost shoe. Fish guts. My lost fishing pole. Nodding to sleep in Marty's Jeep on the way home.

"It's not fair," I mumbled.

"Few are the fair, many are the cruel," a voice said.

I whipped around. The picture fell from my fingers and landed facedown on a lump of dirty clothes.

A red glow framed the case on my bed. I scrambled over to it and knelt on the floor.

"Talia?" I whispered.

The only response was a song. It trickled out like an embarrassed whisper. I rested my chin on my mattress and squinted into the light. A space appeared between the case and my bed, just a sliver at first, then a crack. Then, a gulf opened between the case and my bed as the case floated into the air. It hovered several feet from the bed, compelling me to stand.

The song gained pace and volume. It became a defiant chant. The words sounded as before, unknown; but there was a change in texture, a difference in feeling. Thundering drums took center stage. The weeping strings were barely audible. It pushed me, pumped me, made me want to punch.

The red glow brightened. It radiated in waves, from auburn to cardinal to rose. Raspberry to scarlet to wine, it washed over my room like a red tide.

The case began to spin, slowly at first, like the hands of a clock, then faster and faster. Like kids on a tilt-a-whirl, round and round it turned, nausea be danged. Just as it began spinning so fast it started to generate wind, the whole thing stopped. Lights, song, spinning case, all of it ended.

A shiver of color flashed once, twice across the room. The case plunked to the bed. I looked over my shoulder, again wondering if I was the only witness. Of course I was; the door was still locked.

As I lifted the case, the stone dropped clean out and bounced on my bed.

CHAPTER 31

It never occurred to me that the stone might be different on its backside. I figured it would be round and gray, or like the first side I'd seen – purplish grey, speckled with white and black.

It was not.

The other side of the stone had a triangular impression dead center. It looked like the top of a fedora. And it was in that impression; in that dent, that everything was different.

It was moving. It was agitated. Not the stone, just the center, just that triangular indentation. A swirling, swimming cyclone of blood red and angry white. A twisting, twirling tornado of storm black and sea foam green. A whirling, whipping wind of rusty sand and violent violet.

I whistled and paced before the stone. Its energy was contagious. I rubbed my head and turned round and round, overcome by expectation.

The stone continued to storm. It was as though a mini-micro-climate existed in there, like a world in a space no bigger than a boxing glove. I stuck in my hand. It fit. And then, everything went blinding crystal white, like the sun reflecting off the freshest snow.

It pulled me in.

Or was I pushed?

The swirling vortex rushed all around me, filling the room. It was like I'd pulled the plug on a giant bathtub and I was headed down the drain. Nothing could stop it. Part of me didn't want it to.

A piercing cry flooded my ears. It enveloped me.

I landed on soft, cool grass. The most unusual mixture of aromas – orange blossoms, brownies, wet leather – filled my nostrils. I breathed it in, once, twice.

A phalanx of green dots zoomed over me, high in the cloudless sky.

"How did he get here?" A voice not much different from mine whispered.

"Talia let him in, did she?" another asked.

"That's why she got reprimanded. Almost banished."

I stood to my feet and spun around in halting jerks.

I couldn't see anyone, which was actually not surprising, though it was probably not a good thing that I was growing accustomed to hearing voices.

I shielded my eyes with my hand and studied the horizon. Tall, wavy amber grass stretched out before me on all sides. No houses. No buildings. No cars. No roads. No people. To my left, a far piece away, was a single large tree. It rose like a giant mushroom with an enormous dark canopy. Between where I stood and the giant tree was nothing but a field of light brown. It reminded me of the Great Plains, which I'd never visited, but had seen in my school books.

"Where the heck am I?" I called out. "Dad? Mom?" For some reason I added, "Charlie?"

"You are in Celesteria," a deep voice to my right said.

"Cele-what?" I replied. "Where are y-y-you? Who – What are-are-are you?"

"Celesteria," the voice repeated. "Cel-a-stair-ee-a. Rhymes with hysteria, which I presume you are beginning to feel. Want to try and spell it?" The voice chuckled.

My skin tightened. My stomach gurgled.

"I can't, I can't s-s-s-see you," I said.

"Here I am."

The tall grass began to fold in on itself about a dozen yards away. An invisible mower pressed it down in a zigzag pattern until it stopped at my feet and I could see the informative creature who was speaking.

Just above knee-high to me and stocky as a tree

stump, a chiseled little man stood before me. More Hercules than Adonis, his square face was bookended by a coarse brown beard and furrowed forehead. Though quite short, he was not dwarfish or even gnomish. He was perfectly proportioned, except for his eyes and ears.

His eyes nearly swallowed his face, black bulbs staring at me. His ears were nearly invisible, tiny pellets of flesh stuck on the sides of his head like an afterthought.

I stepped back, nearly tripping over myself. My eyes blinked rapidly, my heart raced.

"What – Who are y-y-y-you?" I asked when I finally was able to speak.

"I am Rashquine, son of Xershmile, of the house of Raquinot." He bowed his head and swept his hands out wide. "May Raquinot live forever," he said, as his head remained bowed. He touched the ground with one knee then stood upright.

A bolt of lightning flashed across the sky.

I looked up. There were no clouds anywhere.

"Strange," I said.

"You will discover much in this land to be a puzzling conundrum. Indeed, you are not alone in that predicament. All things are not without purpose, no matter your perception. Strangeness is not in the object seen but in the eye of the seer. First things first, however, I told you my name. And yours?" He placed his hand on his heart and nodded.

"My n-n-name is Atlas," I replied. "Atlas Forman, fr-fr-fr-from Pinesburg."

"Strange," he said.

"Excuse me?"

"Atlas Forman, you say? Of Pinesburg? Kentucky? Earth?" He rapidly spat out the words, as though he didn't like to hear them. Or say them.

"Yes, th-th-that's right," I answered. "What do you mean by 'Earth'? Is this a different planet? Is this real?"

He smiled, revealing long pointed teeth, longer than I'd have guessed given his slight mouth. He inspected me as he slowly walked in a broad circle. I looked down at him and returned the favor.

A brass cap covered the top of his head, with leather straps hung loosely alongside his thick jaw. His feet were covered in what appeared to be walnut shells, green and firm and dimpled. He wore a sleeveless canvas vest, studded with dark beads. His beef slab upper arms were banded with a wide bronze cuff. A thick coating of coarse dark hair made his ruddy skin appear nearly black.

"Well, Rash-Rash-Rashquine," I said. "Where am I?"

He stroked his chin and looked up at me. He crossed his arms over his abrupt chest and pursed his lips.

"You are sure?" He asked.

"Sure of what?" I squinted at him.

"You are Atlas Forman? The Atlas that everyone's buzzing about?"

"I don't know about people – er, whatever you are – b-b-b-buzzing. B-B-B-But my n-n-name is Atlas Forman. Yes, that's me."

"Funny. I thought you'd be bigger."

"Don't know if I'd be-be-be making cr-cr-cracks about someone's size if I were you," I replied.

I stood straight and planted my fists on my hips as I looked down at him.

"Now, are y-y-you going to tell-tell me where I am? What y-y-y-you are?" I stomped my foot near his to make my point.

He stepped back and folded his hands behind his back.

"My name is Rashquine, son of Xershmile. And I," he paused and stood on his toes. "I am of the house of Raquinot. You are in Celesteria. And you are most unwelcome!"

Suddenly, he jerked both hands from behind his back and swiped at me with a short metal blade. It gleamed as it flashed near my loose-fitting t-shirt.

Just before he plunged it into my soft stomach, I dodged and staggered backward.

"What-what are you d-d-d-doing?" I shouted.

"Ending your destiny before it begins!" He shouted. He roared a terrifying gurgling growl, so deep and violent it shook the ground. "REPHARIAMISI ATTACK!"

He pounced and swung his blade-wielding fist wildly.

I jumped to avoid the stab. As he launched toward me, suddenly, a half dozen of his kind burst from the tall grass all around me, diving at my body, blades drawn.

They surrounded me, growling and hissing, a ring of short frightening rage. Their squat bodies trembled in anger. Saliva dripped from their thick lips as they gnashed their long teeth at me. Rashquine dove at me again and this time, I kicked him, scoring a direct hit against his heavy frame. He tumbled backward, but the others kept moving toward me.

I whirled around and around, hands up to defend myself. There was no way out. As they closed in, the stench of body odor mingled with blood invaded my nostrils. They were mere inches away when I was overcome by an overwhelming urge to shout. From somewhere within, deep within, a fiery sensation ravaged my being. Every bone, every joint, every fiber was filled with a surge of boldness that caused me to erupt with a force I'd never before known. Like my moment with Big Harold and the note, only magnified hundreds of times over. From the soles of my feet, through my skinny legs, up my spine, and out of my mouth flew all the power and fury of a hundred warriors.

"STOP! LEAVE ME BE!" I yelled, as raw and loud as the blast crew's dynamite in the coal mines.

A terrific explosion followed, like an invisible wave. The Rephariamisi tumbled backward and bounced along the ground, rolling head over tail into the weeds.

My body was shaking. A sudden stillness filled the air, like the world after a terrible storm. I turned around and around, scanning the horizon. The Rephariamisi were somewhere in the weeds. Whether they would return was not something I wanted to wait to discover. In the distance, that solitary tree beckoned. It was so familiar yet off putting, like meeting a good friend in a hospital. I wasn't sure if my eyes could be trusted. Another moment or two of silence passed followed by the rustle of grass and a moaning sound. That was all the motivation needed to follow my instinct. I looked toward the tree far away and ran.

Blades of wheat stung my arms as I churned through the field. I had barely reached full speed when the wedge of bright green dots returned in the air above me. They dropped from the sky, growing larger and larger until they were no longer green dots.

I lurched and lost my balance in the tall wet grass. Down I went, a clumsy tumble into the thin stalks. When I stopped rolling, my head was pounding. Sweat rolled down my cheeks into the black soil. I lay flat on my back, spread eagle.

CHAPTER 32

Directly over my face were a dozen Talia's. Well, creatures that looked like they were part of her family, anyway. They wore matching green smocks with white lace trim. Closest to me was a female wearing a large diamond pendant anchored by four silver balls. It dangled just above me as she floated over my eyes.

"T-T-Talia?" I asked.

"No," she replied. Her lambent eyes, lemon yellow and dashed about with sparks of emerald and gold, drew me to my feet.

"I am not Talia," she said. "I am Avila, daughter of Barthomana, of the great house and lineage of Thester."

She turned to the other Apharmari floating behind

her.

"Capture the enemy who assaulted the Ekyllion. Our Ekyllion," she ordered.

Avila held the pendant to her lips and blew into one of the silver balls. All but one of the others streaked into the sky until they were once again green blurs.

Avila's narrow face was framed by voluminous white hair, bundles of curls that bounced as she spoke. Her voice was calm, clear. She was regal and royal; the embodiment of poise.

Bobbing behind her, the one Apharmari who remained smiled demurely. Dressed in a similar green smock, she did not have the pendant. Her dark straight hair was a direct contrast to Avila's locks. The deferential air of servitude emanated from her. She stared at Avila while we spoke.

"Eky, er, Ekyl...what?" I asked. "Talia used that word. And it was in the book. What does it mean?" My adrenaline dissipated, fear redoubled. My hands trembled.

"Relax, Atlas." She drifted closer until we were eye to eye. "Talia shattered the rules and imperiled the order of all things. But, her motives were pure, which is why she still lives."

"What do you mean?" I interjected.

"We will discuss that at another time. Since she opened a door, I must now close it. But, before you go, I will give you some guidance. It is unfair for you to assimilate back to Earth without instruction, without some explanation. I am your Renall Benji – loosely translated it means spirit sister. But is much more than that. I am an Apharmari, a guardian of the dreamers. Many creatures that abide here exist in shadow form on Earth. The creatures of Celesteria and the creatures of Earth have a shared beginning, and by Phillion's glory, we will have a shared ending."

"I'm sorry," I replied. "I don't get what you mean. Who is we? What is the shadow form?"

"Hold out your hand, Atlas."

I lifted my palm. My eyes closed as I hunched my shoulders.

"Fear not!" she declared.

I instantly stood ramrod straight.

She drifted down to my palm and alighted, just as Talia had done the day before. Avila's touch was soothing and electric all at the same time. Her touch filled me with courage. It was palpable, like plunging my arm into a pool of icy water. It was like the cool sensation of anesthesia being infused through an IV. Unlike the anesthesia, this sensation didn't make me drowsy. Quite the contrary, I felt more alive than any moment in my short life.

"Wow," I breathed.

"Now," she said, "it is yet not time for your arrival. How did you transport to Celesteria?"

"What do you mean time for my arrival?" I asked.

The cooling sensation rippled through my body. Wave after wave of energy flooded me, from my extremities to my innards, and back again.

"Atlas, now is not the time for questions. Now is the time for you to return to Earth. To return home." Her brow tightened as her eyes locked on mine. The dazzling array of colors in her eyes – yellow, green, silver, and gold – mesmerized me. I nodded in submission.

"How did you get here?" she asked.

I explained about the case Wyatt and I dug up and the red glow and the song and the book and the stone. I told her how the room spun and everything got sucked into a brilliant light and then I was suddenly in this field.

In Celesteria.

"…And then this little beast dude attacked me," I finished.

"Yes. He is a Rephariamisi. Our enemy. *Your* enemy. His singular desire is to demolish our world, and in so doing, eradicate Human. You arrived through a Harpazzo stone. One of only seven that remain from the dozens created in the aftermath of the Eternal Truce, before the Necessary Dream. Your premature discovery of the case has elevated the intensity of our conflict, but it does not change the mission. Nothing is accidental."

"But, but, I don't underst…"

"Quiet," she cut me off. "As you return, you must remember these two rules. One," she held up a single slender finger, draped in a glittering white glove, "*Nothing is accidental.* Two," she added her middle finger, "*Anything is possible.*"

"But, but, but," I sputtered.

Again she cut me off. "Speak no more. All will be revealed in time. *Through time.*" She beckoned to her fellow Apharmari.

"This is Suseria. She is in her first year of training at the Hall of Instruction. She will take you to your departure."

Suseria floated to me and hovered beside Avila. Avila placed her hands on Suseria's narrow shoulders. They touched foreheads and placed a hand on each other's chest.

"May Phillion be pleased," they whispered simultaneously.

"Let us depart," Suseria spoke, turning to face me. Her voice was warm, almost humid. Words dripped out of her mouth. She pulled the hem of her knee-length smock up, revealing a dagger strapped to her thigh. She unbuckled the clasp and grabbed the ivory-handled blade and slid it out, holding it firmly in her right hand.

"Be safe," Avila said.

"Where are we going?" I asked.

"Not far," Suseria answered. "See that mounded shape just there?"

She pointed to a low hill about half a mile away.

"Yes," I answered.

"That's it. Now run!" She ordered. She began to zoom

215

across the top of the grass. Startled, I looked at Avila.

"Have no fear, I'll be watching. I'm always watching," she said. "Now, Go!"

At her order, I sprang into action and sprinted after Suseria. I swung my arms vigorously, pumping with all my might to keep up with my sky-walking escort.

The cooling sensation I'd felt from Avila intensified. My body felt fluid and fierce. I blurred through the grass faster than I'd ever run in my life. The wind surged around me, whistling in my ears.

We neared the mound. Like the stone in the case, it was purplish-gray with black and white speckles and streaks. Unlike the stone in the case, it did not appear hard. It looked like a massive lump of elephant flesh.

As we got closer I realized it was not a mound. It was not really a hill, either. It was like a hive, with dozens, maybe hundreds of Apharmari swirling about. They flit from spot to spot, like hummingbirds, carrying papers and weapons and food. Some were repairing the hive, spreading lavender cream like drywall spackling. Others moved from point to point in formation, like they were in military training.

Suseria slowed, and I was glad to be able to walk. We continued to move through the field, closing in on the active group of Apharmari.

As we drew nearer, I could hear them singing. It was the song I'd heard coming from the case in my room.

"That song," I said.

"Yes," Suseria answered. "We always sing. Hope has a song. Faith has a song. *Life has a song.* As long as we live, we will sing. As long as we sing, we will live."

She drifted down to my eye-level. She looked at me strongly, her eyes dancing flames of maroon and cobalt.

"Follow me," she said, "but do not speak."

I made a zipping motion with my fingers across my lip.

"Come," she ordered.

I followed her around the edge of activity. She kept us far enough away that I wouldn't be tempted to speak. Or maybe tempted to touch. As we rounded the right side of the hive, I saw multiple smaller hives, scattered throughout the plain.

"Wow," I said.

"Shhh!" Suseria said.

"Sorry," I replied.

"Shhh!"

We reached the edge of the tall grass and stepped onto a muddy patch. Suseria held up her hand for me to stop.

She went a few feet further and clapped her hands three times. Four male Apharmari appeared from the backside of a smaller hive. They were clad in burgundy ankle-length cloaks, fastened with gold tassels from neck to knee. They were stationed at four corners, each holding the end of a pole. Across the two poles was balanced a dark gray piece of slate. They drifted to the ground, gently placing the slate on the soft earth.

"Step forward, Atlas." Suseria said.

I obeyed her command and walked to the slate. Resting on top was a stone, just like the one I'd found in the case.

"I believe you know what to do," Suseria said.

I nodded and gulped hard.

I stood before the blinding hurricane inside the stone. It raged and fumed, in a strange way, inviting me in.

The four Apharmari guards who had carried the stone out now began uncoiling a black tube. They stretched it out, longer than the longest snake I'd seen, and placed it next to the stone.

They came so close to me I couldn't resist. I couln't hold my tongue.

"Hello? What are your names?" I asked.

They didn't respond. Three of them floated back to their position. One remained. He looked at me but said nothing.

"They are positioning the seal of the harpazzo stone," Suseria explained, "as you leave, it will follow and close the portal that you accessed. It should never have opened for you. But, Phillion must have his reasons."

"So, I can't come back here?"

"Do you want to?" Suseria asked.

"I'm not sure." I stared once more at the chaotic swirl inside the stone. "But, I feel a connection here. I feel empowered here." A new thought suddenly popped in my head. "My voice. I have a voice here. Does that make sense?"

"Of course. You sense things you cannot express and you know things you cannot understand. Your voice is just the manifestation of the things yet to be. It would be wonderful to explain more, but it is your time to leave."

She held up her hand like a crossing guard. No more conversation would be had.

"Today you go in peace," she said. "One day, you will return for war. Between now and then, prove your mettle. Think without doubt. Walk without hesitation. Speak without fear. Atlas Forman, your destiny awaits. Remember, nothing is accidental. Anything is possible."

Her face was hardened, her eyes intense. She nodded.

I nodded. It was time to go.

I thrust my hand into the swirling colors. In an instant, the world went time warp white. I spun and spun until my body felt flattened. In another instant, I bounced off the floor in my room.

CHAPTER 33

"Atlas, Atlas. Come on down, pizza's here!"

I looked up at my bedroom ceiling. Solid white except for the chunk of punctured drywall from the time Charlie had thrown a football tee like a throwing star. I stared at it, remembering his constant athletic activity. Wherever we were, he was always moving, jumping, throwing. It was in him. It was him.

Mom had been talking about patching that hole in the ceiling for six months. Now that Charlie was gone, it will never be repaired. After the fact appreciation, I suppose.

I felt light, airy, like my whole body was in a bubble. I stood to my feet, buoyant and bouncy, like my insides were hollow. For the first time since Charlie died, I was all right with him being gone. Not all right as in it wasn't still painful, but all right as in it was something I couldn't change.

"Atlas! You coming?"

"Coming Dad," I yelled.

I shoved my hand in my pocket to check. The note was still there. I pulled it out.

Need to protect it, I thought. *Can't keep wadding it up like a cheat sheet for a math quiz.*

I stepped to my bed. The case was there, just as it had been, open wide, face down. The stone was there, no longer purple and white and shiny. No more hurricane of color soup in a stone bowl, it was just a stone. I placed the letter at the head of my bed and then lifted the stone.

I stared at it, expecting something to happen. Nothing did. I turned it over and over and over again. I rubbed it. Nothing happened. It was just a stone. I set it down and flipped the case over. *Archives of Celesteria.*

My mind raced with questions.

Was it real? It had to be.

What did it all mean? What were those creatures?

What was the connection to Earth? To me?

I did want to go back there. My heart was pounding.

Suddenly, my door was pounding. Well, someone was pounding on my door.

"Atlas? What are you doing?" Dad asked.

"Be right th-th-there, Dad."

"Hurry up. Pizza's getting cold. Mom's home. She wants to talk about the spelling bee."

"Ok. I'm hurrying, I p-p-promise."

I slid the stone into place and brushed the velvet lining with a couple swipes of my hand.

"Gonna read you tonight," I said, turning to the book.

I grabbed Charlie's note. "You too," I whispered. "Every night."

I slid the note into the front of the book and tucked it into its spot in the case. I shut the case and slid it under my bed.

"Okay Dad," I walked out of my room. "Bring on that sausage, onion and mushroom pizza!"

CHAPTER 34

Mom, Dad, Hannah, and Meemaw were already seated around the kitchen table. I guess we still weren't ready to eat in the dining room.

Mom had tears in her eyes as I crossed the threshold from the hallway into the kitchen.

"I'm sorry dear," Dad was trying to console her. "I didn't think it would make you sad. I didn't even realize. I thought it was Atlas's favorite." He looked up at me as I entered.

"Why didn't you say something, Atlas?" Dad asked, clearly perturbed.

"Uhh, I didn't. I don't –"

Mom's halting voice cut me off. "I can't. Eat it. I. Just.

Can't. Reminds me. Friday nights. Football. Celebrating. Charlie. I just. Oh, Preston!" She dropped her head onto her folded arms on the table.

Hannah slid away from her seat and grabbed her toy doll from the corner. She squeezed it under her chin. Its frayed curls darkened from years of floor dragging, spots of moisture now joined the caked-on dirt as Hannah's silent tears dripped down.

She waddled slowly toward me. Her doll was pinned between her elbow and her side, and she softly pushed her hands together and looked up at me. Her blue eyes shimmered under the tears. I pulled her close and held her tight.

"Meredith, honey," Meemaw whispered. She reached across the table and tunneled her hand under Mom's thick hair and sobs. She gently stroked Mom's arm.

Dad stood up and glared at me like it was somehow my fault I didn't tell him that sausage, onion, and mushroom was Charlie's favorite pizza.

"Babe," Dad said. "I really am trying, ok? I'm sorry. Here," he grabbed the red and white checkered cardboard box with *Hot & Fresh Pizza* printed along the edge and carried it to the kitchen counter, "it's gone. Ok? Let's go out for dinner. We could all use a night out. How about Old George's Ribs and Pot Pie Buffet?"

As sad as Mom was feeling, as sad as we all suddenly felt, I almost leaped in the air. Old George's Ribs were so tender and juicy. That tangy sauce and the delicious potpies, chicken, venison; even the catfish potpie was pretty good.

"For once, you've come up with a good idea, Preston," Meemaw said. She leaned back from rubbing Mom's arm. "What do you think, Meredith? It would be good for us to get out of the house."

"Yeah, Mom," I chimed in.

Mom slowly raised her head. Her light blue sleeve was puddled navy blue from a shower of tears and snot.

"Why not?" She slid her nose along the length of her arm, wiping the remaining dribbles away.

"Can I change clothes first?" She asked. Her voice was soft and pained, like it was the morning after one of her triathlons. Like every ounce of strength was gone and there wasn't anything left to do but sit and stare.

"Are you sure you're ok to go?" I asked.

She looked up at me. I stepped back from Hannah's hug and walked to the edge of the table and leaned in. Her blue eyes glistened through a film of tears.

"I'm sure." She sniffed. "Come closer."

I leaned across the table until our noses nearly touched.

"You are a wonderful boy. I'm so proud of you." She patted my head and slowly traced my cheek and chin with the back of her hand.

I gulped.

"Thank you for being you. I am sorry I've been lost. I

promise, I'm coming home. I'm coming home…" her voice trailed off. Her tears returned.

"You never left, Mom." That was all I could get out before my voice got caught somewhere between my lungs and my lips.

"She's right, son," Dad said from the other side of the table.

I felt two small hands grab my waist and a small face burrow into my side, just below my ribs.

I reached down with one arm and held Hannah close. Dad moved behind Mom and placed his hands on her shoulders. Even Meemaw joined the circle of love. She wedged between Hannah and Mom. We were connected. In that moment, everything felt like it was going to be ok.

After a few seconds, Dad cleared his throat.

"If we're going to go to Old George's, we should probably get rolling."

"Sounds goo-goo-good," I said. I couldn't wait to go. Old George's was my favorite place in Pinesburg, maybe in all of Kentucky. It's even better than the Cracker Barrel. Marty said Cracker Barrel was a bunch of sell-outs anyway.

"If you want good eatin'," he would say, "you got to get to a place that's always running out of toilet paper in the men's room."

I had a suspicion about what running out of toilet paper had to do with Marty's version of good eating, but I was afraid to ask.

"Let's do it." Mom said, determination filling her. She stood up and smacked her hands on the table. "I'm ready for a good meal."

"That's the spirit," Meemaw said. "I'll go get my coat."

"Mommy?" Hannah asked.

Mom knelt down and cupped Hannah's chubby face in her hands. "Yes my sweet princess?"

"Can I bring Katie?" She held up her dingy doll, which remained Hannah's favorite despite a lazy eye and a recent arm amputation, courtesy of a neighbor's Rottweiler.

Mom smiled. She smiled bigger than I'd seen in a long time. Or, at least bigger than I'd seen since Charlie died. She scooped Katie from Hannah's arms and tossed the doll in the air. Mom caught her and planted a big kiss on her cheek. She handed Katie back to Hannah and planted an even bigger kiss on Hannah's cheek.

"Of course, Hannah, of course. Why don't you go get Katie's jacket while I go change?"

Hannah took off for the playroom fast as lightning.

Mom walked upstairs to change her clothes.

It was just me and Dad in the kitchen.

"Well, Atlas, guess you and me are the only ones who don't require a wardrobe adjustment to go to dinner."

"Yep."

I leaned against the doorframe between the kitchen and the hallway. Dad stood near the kitchen counter. He turned his attention to the pizza box.

"What are we going to do with this now?" He skid the box back and forth between the sink and the toaster. "I *hate* leftovers."

"I don't mind them," I said.

"But this isn't even the kind of pizza you like." He lifted the lid and sniffed.

"Maybe I could learn to like it," I offered.

"Well, it sure smells good." He turned toward me and took a step. He stood in front of our shiny refrigerator. No childhood drawings or photographs adorned the front. No magnets. Mom liked things clean.

"Speaking of learning to like it," Dad said. "Maybe I could do a better job of learning to like things I haven't liked in the past."

"Might be a lot of things in that category," I said.

"Definitely," he replied as he smiled. "We all grieve differently, huh buddy?"

"Yeah, I think I heard someone smart say that once," I replied.

He took another step and knuckled my hair.

I laughed.

He laughed.

We laughed. Together.

CHAPTER 35

Even though I was starving, the drive to Old George's Ribs and Pot Pies went fast. For the first time since Charlie's accident *everyone* was in good spirits, *at the same time.* As amazing as Celesteria was, part of me worried it was just another daydream. Even if it was real, this moment with my family was real, too. Celesteria would have to wait.

We pulled into the parking lot. The row closest to the door was aglow from *Old George's* familiar crimson neon sign. Its mustard letters flashed like a buoy in the ocean, guiding us to the harbor of yumminess that was a seventy-three item buffet, and the forty-four topping sundae bar. I was ready to feast.

"I'm going to eat a whole bowl of banana puddin',"

Hannah said as she wriggled out of her booster seat.

"Oh, really," Meemaw cackled. "Not if I beat you to it!"

Hannah giggled and slid out of her booster seat.

"Let me park the car first," Dad said with a grin. He looked over at Mom. "I'm awful glad you said yes."

"It's just a restaurant," Mom replied.

As he turned off the family wagon, he leaned over and pecked Mom on the cheek.

"I'm not talking about the restaurant, dear."

"Let's go, let's go," Hannah shouted from right beside my ear. She pushed against my side as hard as she could. Her little fingers tickled my ribs.

"Ok," I laughed. "Hold your horses."

"I'd rather hold 'em than ride 'em," Meemaw said from the other side of the back seat. "My old back couldn't handle all that bouncing around. Nearly killed me riding back here with you kids. Could've slowed down a little around those turns, don't you think, Preston?"

Dad was already outside the car. Hannah climbed over my lap as I opened the door. We spilled out into the parking lot and nearly ran to the front door of the restaurant.

"Welcome to Old George's Ribs and Pot Pies," the teenage hostess said as we walked through the swinging glass doors. We hovered around her check-in stand like a jumble of moths around a porch light.

"Stand still," Dad scolded. "Sorry about them," he

said to the hostess. "Kylie, is it?" He eyed the faded enamel nametag magnetically fixed to her red and yellow Old George's t-shirt.

"Yes sir," Kylie grinned. "Just one kids menu tonight?" she asked, looking at Hannah and me.

"Yes, j-j-just one," I replied as I stood on my tiptoes.

She grabbed four laminated adult menus and a photocopied coloring page. She pulled a couple broken crayons from a small metal bucket behind her.

"Right this way, please."

We were about four steps into the main dining area – a lily pad like arrangement of dark wood ovals, bordered by ketchup and mustard-colored plastic chairs – when she stopped and turned.

"I know you – you ride bus four to PMS, right?"

Everyone looked at me.

"Ye-Ye-Yes, I do."

"Your friend is already here." She turned to Dad. "Did y'all want to sit near them?"

She pointed across the room to a corner booth.

We all looked.

"Old Frank Jamison, why I haven't talked to him in a couple months," Dad said.

"Wendy's here too," Mom added.

It was Wyatt's family. There he sat, with his mom and dad and little brother, all as neat and tidy as a freshly painted fence. Straight and proper, no elbows on the table, eating their dinner.

"Sounds good to me," Dad said.

Kylie led us to the open six-seater table right beside Wyatt's family's booth.

"Hey Frank, how ya been?" Dad backslapped, in full campaign mode.

"Finer than frog hair sliced in half," Frank replied, standing to lock hands with Dad. They stood there, fists pumping in a firm handshake like they were at a college reunion. Made sense, I suppose; they had been frat brothers for one semester at the University of West Virginia.

"Mountaineer pride will keep you alive," Dad used to say. Even though he finished at another college, he acted like he was the biggest Mountaineer booster in the county.

"Hello Meredith, it's nice to see you," Wyatt's mom said.

She didn't ask how Mom was, just that it was nice to see her. Grown-ups have ways of saying things like that. Of course, not that anyone wanted Mom to say how bad she was feeling and start blubbering all over the place in the middle of Old George's buffet.

"Nice to see you, Wendy," Mom replied. Dad and Wyatt's dad decoupled and we all sat at our table.

"Wyatt, you want to go eat dinner with your buddy," his dad offered. "They got an extra place at the table."

Wyatt looked at me. I grinned and scooped my hand, motioning for him to come over. *Hoping* he'd come over.

232

He slid out from the booth and walked around to the spot at the far end of our table. I sat kitty-corner to him, and Meemaw sat across from me.

"My name's Tommy, I'll be takin' care of y'all tonight," a greasy-haired, middle-aged man said. He tossed faded red paper drink coasters around the table and then started to go down on one knee, pen in hand. He stopped halfway down, winced in pain and stood back up.

"Trick knee," he said. "Tough getting old, ya know what I mean?"

"Sure is," Dad answered.

"Anyway," Tommy continued. "What can I get y'all to drink?"

We all gave our drink orders.

"Everybody getting the buffet tonight?" Tommy asked.

We all nodded our heads.

"All right then, just help yourself whenever you're ready. And you might want to hurry, the sweet potato casserole is going fast tonight." Tommy chuckled and limped away.

Wyatt looked at me then looked at Meemaw. Obviously, he wasn't going to talk about our friendship, whatever was left of it, in front of her. I took the hint.

"Hey Meemaw, you better hustle if you want to get that sweet potato casserole. Or, better yet, beat Hannah to that banana pudding," I said.

"You know that's right," Meemaw said. She smiled

at me. "Don't worry, though, I know what I'm doing. I may have been born at night, but it wasn't last night."

She pushed back from the table and pulled a small plastic container out of her giant purse.

"Perfect little place to store an extra helping for my late night snack," she winked at us and walked off to the buffet.

Mom and Hannah were long gone, piling their plates high with an assortment of heat-lamp-warmed food. Dad and Frank were yucking it up at the other end of the table, oblivious to anyone else.

"Wyatt," I said, wasting no time, "I'm sorry about the other day in school, and I'm really really sorry about not showing up that morning to get Big Harold, but…"

"Atlas," he cut me off. He leaned on the table and held up an open hand to quiet me.

"I've been thinking," he continued. "How long have we been friends? Best friends?"

"Since first grade. Since I dumped glue down the little Brewster kid's shirt after he pushed you after reading circle. We were reading *Frog and Toad are Friends*. Ha! I still remember thinking that you were like Frog and I was like Toad."

Wyatt smiled. "I'm like Frog, huh? Wasn't he the one that tricked Toad into thinking it was spring time by ripping months off the calendar?"

"Oh, yeah, I remember th-th-that," I replied.

"Well," Wyatt sat up straight. "I think you're the one playing tricks. Maybe you're Frog and I'm Toad. At least with that book you claim to be able to read."

"I'm telling you," I said as I slapped the table, "it's real!"

"Everything all right boys?" Mom asked as she lifted Hannah into her seat. Hannah's plate was covered in a mass of yellow and white, with a sprinkle of green and orange, just enough peas and carrots to offset the glob of banana pudding.

"Yes Mom, everything's good," I replied.

"Well, y'all better get your dinner."

"Ok, Mom."

Wyatt waited for my mom to start chatting with his mom before continuing the conversation.

"Look Atlas," Wyatt whispered, "What I'm trying to say is we've known each other too long and been through too much for me to end our friendship because I can't see what you can. You've always seen things differently from the rest of the crowd. No reason for me to be upset about this book. Just keep it between us, ok?"

"Ok, on one condition?" I asked.

"Sure, name it," Wyatt replied.

"You agree to come over tomorrow night and see the weird st-st-stone. And hear about everything th-th-that happened. And you listen to it all without j-j-j-judging or ending our friendship."

"That's three things," Wyatt laughed.

"Ok, three things. Agreed?"

"Agreed."

I nodded and looked down, studying the flecks of knife marks that scarred the solid inch of lacquer coating the cinnamon colored table.

Wyatt rolled his knife handle across his palm.

After a few moments of not looking at each other, and realizing we'd made amends, I looked at Wyatt.

"You're a true friend," I said.

"You too," Wyatt replied.

"Hey," he elbowed me in the upper arm. "How about we get some of that sweet potato casserole?"

CHAPTER 36

That night at Old George's was the best night in a long time. We pigged out. Meemaw ate so much she passed out, and at nearly every red light on the way home, Mom and Dad made out. That last part wasn't what made it the best night. Hannah and I covered our eyes. Meemaw snored. But, it was good to see them getting along. Real good.

In between stoplights and over-the-top kisses, Mom asked about the spelling bee.

"Atlas, I'm sorry, we haven't had a chance to talk. Dad said you were going to be in the spelling bee that happens in a couple weeks. And, if you do good enough, you will compete this summer? I can hardly believe it. How was the practice?"

Dad was so proud, he didn't give me a chance to respond.

"Meredith, the kid's a genius!" he exclaimed. "He spelled words I didn't even know. Maybe he's going to law school one day, like his old man! Still got a little work on that tricky stutter, but I think he's close. Don't you, Atlas?"

It felt good to hear Dad's praise. Real good. I still didn't want to go through with the spelling bee, but every cloud has a silver lining. If the spelling bee meant that I wouldn't get suspended from school, and I didn't have to tell Mom and Dad about saying the "F" word and fighting Big Harold, and if it meant Dad would actually look at me with some measure of pride, then it was worth it.

"I th-th-think so," I replied.

"I'm so glad, Atlas. I'm so proud of you. When's your next practice?" Mom asked.

"After school tomorrow."

"I can't wait to see you in action," Mom said.

Dad turned up the radio.

"I like seeing you in action," Dad whispered to Mom. Then he made a disgusting low growl out the corner of his mouth.

I guess he thought we couldn't hear him. I hope he thought we couldn't hear him. But we could. It's surprising how often grown-ups think kids aren't listening. We're *always* listening.

We weren't in the garage five seconds and I was already running into the house to go up to my room.

"Good night, Atlas, we love you," Mom called out as I streaked through the kitchen.

"Good night, everyone, l-l-l-love you too," I replied. I was down the hallway and halfway up the stairs before anyone else even got out of the car.

I slipped into my room and pulled the door closed.

Finally, it was time to read the book from Celesteria.

I dropped to the floor and slid my hands under my bed, inching along until I felt the now familiar hardened metal frame of the Celesteria case. My fingers slid around its smooth edges and I gripped it tightly and dragged it out from under the bed.

It was so smooth. How old was Celesteria? How old was the Earth? I rubbed the trim that separated the two halves. I flipped the case over and sat up, crisscross applesauce.

Crazy. It was too real to be a daydream. Wasn't it?

I sat alone, twitching with excitement. Time to open it up and read. Time to find out what it says about Celesteria and Earth and the Necessary Dream and the Ekyllion and the floating creatures and…

I turned it over in my hand, trying to find an opening. As I kept fumbling with the case, I remembered the night we found it. There was no latch. There was no handle or keyhole or other way to open it.

"NO!" I screamed. My mind flooded with the image of shutting the case when Dad was banging on the door for me to come eat pizza. The case was closed.

I had closed it.

I held the case up to my ear and shook it. No noise. No rattle. No banging of stone against book.

"No, no, no!" I screamed again.

"Atlas, what's wrong?" Meemaw asked from the hallway. "Is everything ok? Are you all right?"

She pushed the door open. She stood in the threshold, hands on her hips, worry in her eyes.

"I don't know, Meemaw." *And I forgot to lock my door.*

"What happened? I was reading to Hannah and heard you screaming. Did you fall or somethin'?"

She entered my room and stepped over the clutter like so many land mines. She swung my desk chair around and wheeled it as far as she could toward me. A mound of dirty clothes served as a roadblock. She was forced to stop pushing the chair before she could get any closer to my spot on the bedside rug.

"Might not fall if you cleaned up a little, huh?" She asked as she plopped down in my desk chair.

"I suppose. I didn't f-f-f-fall, though," I replied.

"I haven't been in this room in a long time." She looked around. As she did, her left hand trembled on the padded armrest. "I remember when I was a little girl, for a couple years this room was where your grand uncle stayed.

He was sick a lot, but I remember he had the craziest imagination. Like someone else I know." She winked at me.

"My grand uncle?" I asked.

"Yes, your daddy's Uncle Benjamin, your Grandpa Forman's brother. You never met him. He was a character, though, a real head-in-the-clouds kind of kid. We all went to school together. Everybody knew everybody back then, back when Pinesburg was tiny." She looked toward the ceiling. Her hand shimmied a little harder, causing the chair frame to squeak.

"It's not exactly a b-b-big city now, Meemaw."

"True," she replied, still staring at the ceiling. "Maybe it wasn't the population. It was the attitude. People just knew each other better. We didn't have all the computers and phones and stuff, creating barriers between everybody."

"I understand."

"What are you holding in your lap?" She asked without looking down.

I looked down at the case.

"Oh, n-n-n-nothing," I answered.

"Atlas Michael Forman," she said, her eyes dropping from the plain white drywall overhead to give me a stare.

"Don't push me down the stairs and tell me I tripped."

"Well, it's uh," I began.

"Give it here." She looked me in the eye. She held out her wrinkled hands, palms up.

"Uh, umm," I muttered. I looked at the dirty tube

socks and the balled-up t-shirts between us.

"It's kind of a big deal," I said. "I really haven't shown anyone."

"I'm not just anyone, Atlas. I'm your Meemaw, remember?"

"I know. It's j-j-j-just that," I said.

"It looks old and dirty. Is it a buried treasure? You afraid your old Meemaw is going to steal your gold?" She stood up and walked back to the doorway. She closed the door and turned the inset doorknob lock.

"Atlas, you can trust me. I'm not going to tell anyone," Meemaw said as she walked toward me. "Besides, at my age, people are used to me saying crazy stuff. They wouldn't believe me anyway."

She walked around the pile of dirty clothes.

"Help me out," she said.

She started crumbling to the floor. I slid the case to the floor and placed her hands on my shoulders to brace her drop.

"Been a long time since I sat on the floor," she wheezed.

"Yeah," I said, "l-l-like s-s-s-since I was a little boy."

"You're still a little boy."

"I'm in seventh grade, you know," I replied.

"Yes. Whew, that took it out of me. Now I'm down here and your Mom won't let me smoke in the house. You better do something to make this worth it. I'm all wore out like John Henry's forearms."

I leaned back as she settled on the rug. Her leaky eye was red and draining. Her gaze, though, was firm and fixed. I'm pretty sure it twinkled.

"Everybody knows you're smart, Meemaw. Ain't nobody gonna think you are crazy. I w-w-will tell you. B-B-But, you gotta swear on Marty's gr-gr-grave…"

She interrupted me. "Why Marty's grave? You always liked him, didn't ya?"

I smiled. "Yeah. I m-m-mean I loved Grandpa, too, I just,"

She interrupted me again. "Of course, honey. But Marty was awful keen on you. He took a shine to you from the first day y'all met."

"I reckon."

"You still got that picture from the fishing trip in here?" Meemaw asked, craning her neck toward the bookshelf in the corner of my room. "Oww," she winced and rubbed her neck. "Truth be told, I don't know how much longer I got on this here Earth. Truth on a stack of Bibles, I don't know how much longer I want."

"Oh, Meemaw," I replied. "Don't say that. I'll get the picture for you."

"Don't bother right now, honey," she replied as I started to stand. "Just tell me about that case."

She wasn't going to relent.

"Ok," I said. I knelt on the floor and slid the case in

front of her. "Problem is, I can't ope-ope-open it. At least not when I w-w-w-want to."

Meemaw lifted the case. She held it at arms' length, quivering as she kept it suspended between us. She was wearing her half-glasses and the gold chain drooped across her neck trembled as she spoke.

"What do you make of this, Atlas? You can't open it? But, it's been open before?"

"Yes, Meemaw. It's the most incredible thing ever."

"Really?" She set it on the floor. Her ancient hands fingered every square inch of the ancient case.

"Quit acting like a squirrel in wintertime, Atlas. Tell your Meemaw. What happened?"

"Ok. You pr-pr-pr-promise not to tell anyone?"

She just grimaced and tilted her head.

"Ok. I know you w-w-won't. Well, Meemaw, there's a book and a stone in there, from another world. From a place called –"

"Celesteria," she interrupted.

I fell back against my bed.

Had Meemaw heard about it before?

Did she know about it?

Did my grand Uncle Benjamin visit Celesteria?

Did Meemaw visit Celesteria?

"How'd you know that?" I asked, my heart racing.

"I read the case, silly," she replied.

"Oh. Right. Well, the stone is like a transporter. I went

to Cel-Cel-Cel-Celesteria. There's these creatures that fly –
well, they kinda just hover – and they are like guardians of
mankind. And there was these other creatures that tried to
kill me, and…"

I went on and on, telling Meemaw everything. Every
detail erupted out of me like a shook-up soda can.

After a solid five minutes of machine gun talking that
left me nearly breathless, Meemaw asked a question.

"You sure this isn't one of your daydreams? Maybe
with all the stress and everything that's been happening…"

"No. I don't think so. I mean, no. That's why I wish I
could open the case. Mee-Mee-Meemaw, I'm really s-s-s-
sure it was real."

"Ok, ok, don't get upset, honey," Meemaw said. She
placed her trembling hand on my arm.

"If only I could open the case. Then you'd see," I said,
"then Wyatt would believe me. I just want someone to
believe me." The familiar warmth of my blushing cheeks
returned. My throat felt hot as I fought tears.

"I just want one person to believe me. F-F-For once
in my life. I'm tired of fe-fe-f-feeling like I'm all alone. Like
I'm th-th-the only one."

Meemaw's hand crept down to mine. She clasped
mine in hers, a jumble of warped knuckles sandwiching
adolescent smoothness.

"Look at me, Atlas."

I lifted my eyes until ours met.

"Remember this, Atlas." The intensity in her eyes stopped my heart. I held my breath.

"You say you're the only one who believes?"

I nodded.

"It only takes *one person believing* to make it so."

CHAPTER 37

Meemaw's words were still in my head when I woke up. Maybe she was right. I didn't know. I guess the world's full of stuff that was once only believed by one.

One thing was for sure. The case was real. And everything I felt, well, it all felt real.

I sat up in bed and looked across at the picture from the fishing trip.

"What do you think, Charlie? Sure wish you were here."

You should be yourself.

I stood to my feet and reached high overhead, stretching my whole body until my tiptoes nearly left the floor.

"Aahhh," I yawned and squeezed my eyes tight as I rocked my head, trying to shake the sleep from my brain.

My glowing digital clock displayed the time, 6:55 AM.

I stuck my nose into my armpit and inhaled.

"Whew!" I definitely needed a shower before heading to the bus. I looked down. The case was sitting on my floor, still as a corpse, and just as lifeless, now that I couldn't open it.

"Wish you'd open up." I knelt down beside it. I shook it and tapped on the thick alloy frame. "Such a mystery. That's no surprise, though. You were buried behind Crankenstein's house, after all."

As I said *Crankenstein*, I saw a glimmer of a red glow through the old window on the back wall of my room, the only one with a view in the direction of Dr. C's place.

"Crankenstein," I said.

Nothing happened. I snapped my fingers in disgust.

"Crankenstein," I said once more.

Maybe it wasn't simultaneous, but within a second or two, the red glow appeared. Maybe Crankenstein was the key?

"Atlas!"

I'm telling Wyatt. I knew Crankenstein had something to do with this.

"Atlas!" Mom was calling.

"Yes, Mom?"

"It's Friday. I can take you to school today." Her voice was full of life. It echoed up the stairs and radiated through my door as bright as a mid-summer sunrise.

"Ok. I'm gonna take a shower," I yelled.

"Ok, dear. And, I'm going to come to your spelling bee practice after school. I can't wait!"

Spelling bee practice. Right. I turned back to the case. "Won't you please open?"

Silence.

"Crankenstein."

No red glow.

I tucked it away, under the head of my bed. I pulled my blankets up and slid my hand along, smoothing out the bigger lumps.

I walked toward the door, hop scotching over the random squares of mess spilled like buckshot all over the floor. Just before opening my door, I looked at the picture again. Charlie's grin was pure. Free.

"You would know how to open the case, wouldn't you Charlie?" I asked as I held the leather frame in my hand.

You should be yourself.

"I know, I know, I should be myself. Whatever that means." I set the picture back on the shelf and grabbed the doorknob. A thought sprang to the front of my mind.

You should be yourself.

Charlie's note.

Charlie's note!

"Dang it!" I rapped my fist against the hollow wooden door. I slumped to the floor and stared beyond the dirty clothes piles. I felt like I couldn't breathe. The only thing I had from my brother. Gone.

"Charlie's note. I p-p-put it in the book. In the case," I whispered.

"Hey son, good morning." Dad walked by the doorway. He stopped and looked down at me quizzically. He was dressed for work already, tip-to-toe in his casual Friday blazer and loafers.

"What are you doing on the floor? Did you say something about Charlie? About the case? The trial is set for July. But, it's a formality. I told you the guy blew a point twenty three when the cops pulled him out of his truck."

I hoped my eyes weren't red. I could feel tears coming but I sure didn't want to try to explain to Dad everything that had happened with the book, the case, and my trip to Celesteria. We were just starting to get along. Last thing I needed was to say something that gave him a reason to revert to "Atlas is a moron" mode. So, I went along with him.

"I know. Sorry, Dad. Sorry to br-br-bring it up."

"It's going to be tough, Atlas. But, I believe we're going to be alright." He walked to the top of the stairs.

I walked to the bathroom across the hall. The bathroom I shared with Hannah, sort of. I used the shower and the toilet, and she got to pick out the decorations and the paint, which meant I showered with pink princesses and unicorns.

"Hey Atlas, wait a sec."

"Yes, Dad?"

I stopped in the bathroom doorway. He stood on the top two steps, leaning on the banister.

"If you want to talk about Charlie, let me know. You can talk to me about him or anything, really, ok?"

"Ok."

"Ok. Have a good day, son."

"Thanks Dad."

CHAPTER 38

Mom had a box of those anti-drunk driving brochures in the front seat, so I sat in the back, across from Hannah. She had a fistful of cereal and a juice box in the door cup holder. Her pudgy legs dangled off her booster and kicked the back of Mom's seat.

"Hannah, dear, please quit kicking," Mom pleaded.

"Sorry Mama."

"It's ok, honey, just try to keep your feet still. Atlas, do you have any tests today?" Mom asked.

I had no idea. Schoolwork was about number six hundred on my list of things to worry about.

"No," I answered.

She turned the radio volume down. Classic country

music was Mom's taking-the-kids-to-school soundtrack. *Alabama, The Oak Ridge Boys and Hank Williams*, among others, escorted us to the old brick school building almost every morning.

"Really? You have no tests on a Friday?"

"Well, not that I can re-re-re-remember." I looked out the window. As she continued talking, we passed two stucco office parks with about a fifty percent vacancy rate, and Brother Westler's church. The white painted wood was splintered and crumbling around the stained glass windows. The blood red front doors were dotted with swarming black mold spores. I changed the subject.

"Hey Mom, how come Dad doesn't really go to church with us? How come we don't r-r-really go much?"

"Miss Whitney says church is God's house. And if we're good, we are s'posed to visit Him," Hannah answered.

"That's true Hannah," Mom said. Her smile in the rearview mirror reinforced the joy in her voice at Hannah's response.

"So, does that mean Dad isn't a g-g-g-good person?" I asked.

"No, Atlas," Mom paused. "Your father is a good person. He just works hard and likes to take it easy on Sunday."

We pulled up to the eight car back-up, blinker ticking, to turn into school. Mr. Hopkins, the retired cop, held up his orange-gloved hand as he waved the cars coming the other direction to enter the parking lot.

"I work hard too," I said.

"Atlas, it's not the *same*," Mom replied.

Everyone grieves differently.

Finally, Mr. Hopkins waved for our row to move. As Mom circled around to the drop-off spot, she turned up the radio. I didn't know the song, but the lyrics were eerily prescient, like the radio was eavesdropping on our conversation. As we gathered our backpacks and slid out the back door, I could hear old Hank Williams, singing for all he was worth.

> *"There's a place near to me, where I'm longing to be*
> *With my friends at the old country church,*
> *There with grandma we went,*
> *and our Sundays were spent,*
> *With our friends at the old country church..."*

CHAPTER 39

There must have been a memo sent around to all the teachers to take it easy that day. Or, maybe they were just as ready for school to end as the students. Either way, half of my classes showed movies and most of the others played games. Even in the Walrus's Civics class, which was always the most serious, we only had to write a short essay about the difference between Federalism and Communism.

I had just finished scribbling about the connection between individual property rights and economic growth when the bell rang.

"All right, class. If you are done, put your paper in Uncle Sam." Sitting on the corner of the Walrus's desk was a ceramic Uncle Sam with a metal basket fixed to the top of its top hat. *I Want YOUR Assignment* was hand-painted across its chest.

"If you haven't finished your essays, you can work on them over the weekend. See you on Monday, Lord willing and the creek don't rise."

As I waited for my turn to drop my paper in the hat, Wyatt scuttled over and stood beside me, backpack on his shoulder.

"I'll be over tonight. Like I promised," he said.

"Oh, r-r-right," I said.

"You want me to come before or after dinner?" Wyatt asked.

All I could think about was that Charlie's note was gone, maybe for good. The case was closed and there was no way to open it. Should I tell Wyatt? No. Maybe it would open again before he came. Or maybe he could help me open it.

That's just wishful thinking, I thought.

"Go ahead and come be-be-before dinner. J-J-Just call first," I finally said.

I flipped the paper onto Uncle Sam. I glanced at the Walrus, whose mouth was stuffed with jalapeno flavored potato chips and whose fist was buried in the gaudy green, red, and white colored plastic bag, grabbing a refill. Wyatt laughed out loud as I followed him through the rows of dull beige desks.

"The Walr-r-r-rus is gr-gr-gross," I whispered.

"For sure," Wyatt replied over his shoulder.

The hall was Friday loud. Kids running, shouting, bumping along, like white blood cells surging to fight an infection on the other side of the double door exit.

A pack of older girls pranced by us, drowning us in their wake of perfume and pubescent pride.

Wyatt's chest popped out.

"Like you h-h-have a ch-chance." I laughed.

"You never know," Wyatt said, once the girls had turned the corner. "I heard that Connor Pike was dating a junior."

"Well," I replied. "He's also like sixteen. He's probably as old as Big Har-Harold."

"Is he still in the hospital?" Wyatt asked.

"Far as I know."

We dodged the teenage traffic until we reached my locker.

"What are you doing tonight?"

"I got spelling bee practice now," I said as I pinched the metal handle and yanked until the door of my locker swung open.

"Oh, right. How'd it go yesterday?" Wyatt asked.

"Actually," I replied as I unloaded my backpack, "I did pretty good." I smiled. I stacked everything in my locker except my spelling workbook and slammed the door shut.

"That's great. Well, have a good practice. I'll give you a call later," Wyatt said.

"Ok."

He walked toward the exit. I walked back toward the classrooms. The hall was suddenly Friday afternoon empty.

"Hey Atlas," Wyatt yelled as he pushed the door open.

"Yeah?" I turned and looked back at him. He was grinning ear to ear, and had turned his hat backwards. At least for Wyatt, the weekend had started.

"I'm really looking forward to seeing what's in that case. Really, I am."

"Cool. S-S-S-See you tonight."

How am I going to get the case opened? I thought as I walked toward the classroom for spelling bee practice.

I have to get Charlie's note.

"Atlas!"

I turned around again. Mom stood in the doorway, holding the door open. "Wait a second. Wait for us."

"Us?" I asked. I leaned against the painted cinderblock wall. "Who's us?" I repeated.

"Dad's parking the car. How was your day?" Mom asked loudly.

"Fine." A good sixty feet separated us and there was something awkward about shouting at each other in the desolate hallway. I didn't want to make her feel bad but I didn't want to continue the conversation this way.

"I'm going to go on to the room, ok? I want to get focused. Dad knows where it is."

"Ok, Atlas. We'll be in there in a minute."

The only sound was the rustling made by the plastic clips on the straps of my backpack as I dragged it along the smudge-streaked floor. I could hear Miss Pendleton talking as I walked into the classroom.

"You can repeat the word, and you can ask questions, but as soon as you begin spelling, you have to finish."

Miss Pendleton was in the same spot as yesterday. She was seated in the metal folding chair, beside Coach Jefferson, pulled up to the plastic table. Two empty chairs were beside the rotund coach.

She wasn't talking to Coach Jefferson, though. On the other side of the table stood another student. A female student.

"Hey Atlas," Aamilah said. She was smiling, which took me by surprise, considering our last conversation.

"He-Hey Aamilah," I replied. "What are y-y-you doing here?" I stood just inside the doorway, backpack still on the ground beside my feet.

"She's going to join us," Miss Pendleton said. She pushed her chair back and stood to her feet. Her hair was cinched up high and tight, drawing my eyes to her graceful neck. The pearl necklace had returned.

"Aamilah is going to be part of the practice session. And," Miss Pendleton waved me in the room, "she may even become a contestant."

I must have smiled a little too widely, because Miss Pendleton laughed.

"Oh, I'm glad to see you don't object to the plan."

"No ma'am." I walked to the table. Miss Pendleton looked behind me.

"Welcome Mr. Forman. And Mrs. Forman! What a pleasant surprise. I'm so glad you all could be here." Miss Pendleton reached to shake hands with my parents as they walked into the room.

I dropped my backpack on the table and circled around Aamilah. Her caramel skin glistened. She was still smiling as I stood at attention on the other side of the podium.

"Sorry I got upset with you the other day," she whispered.

I looked straight ahead. Coach Jefferson and Miss Pendleton were still conversing with Mom and Dad. They were huddled behind the table. Coach was animated. His arms waved about and his jaw flapped open and shut like a saloon door during happy hour.

I looked at Aamilah. "Don't be s-s-s-sorry. You were right."

"Well, I shouldn't have been so rude. You're a nice guy. I don't know what got into me." Her dark eyes danced for a moment, then briefly hid behind her long lashes before popping back out with her smile.

"Is everyone ready to begin?" Miss Pendleton asked.

The adults took their seats. Once again, the firing squad impression was unmistakable. I was excited to be near Aamilah, and to know that she wasn't mad at me. At the same time, I was nervous to be near Aamilah, especially because she was no longer mad at me.

"Yes Miss Pendleton," Aamilah said.

The old clock ticked loudly in the back of the room. Its thick black oval frame and its dull red hands reminded me of Marty's pocket watch that he'd kept in his tackle box. He'd palm it and pop it open to check the time when he was trying new bait.

"If it takes 'em more than five cycles to chomp, you better try something different. Goes for the ladies, too." Then he'd wink and laugh, and grab a handful of night crawlers, picking the mud off before poking them with the hook.

"Atlas? Hello Atlas? Are you ready?" Miss Pendleton asked.

I looked up. Four sets of grown-up eyeballs were boring through me like the hook through that fat juicy worm.

"Yup. Umm, I mean, Y-Y-Yes ma'am."

The practice session went about as smoothly as I'd begun. Between Aamilah and the occasional thought of Wyatt and the un-openable case from Celesteria, and Mom's cheerleading and Coach Jefferson's random sports hyperbole, I struggled to concentrate.

I missed more words than I spelled correctly, almost all because of my stutter. I would've been really upset except for what happened when it was over.

"Well, I'm sure we can do better next week," Miss Pendleton said after I misspelled *glaucophane*, which apparently is a type of bluish black crystal. I started thinking about Wyatt's missing stone and the harpazzo stone that took me to Celesteria.

I wonder if I'll ever go back. If I do, I'm going to have to bring some kind of shield or weapon. Maybe Wyatt will loan me his pocketknife.

"Atlas!" Coach Jefferson shouted, jarring every cell in my body.

"Did you hear Miss Pendleton?" He asked.

"Y-Y-Yes," I said.

"It's ok, honey," Mom said. "You did your best and that's all that matters."

"You'll do better next time, I'm sure," Dad added. "We'll make sure you put in extra time practicing this weekend."

The adults stood and said their goodbyes to each other. Mom and Miss Pendleton gave each other a half hug, while Dad and Coach Jefferson did some kind of fist bump extended congratulatory maneuver like they were football players. I just stood and watched and waited.

Then one of the best things ever happened.

Aamilah turned to me and smiled.

"Maybe we could practice together," she said.

Act calm. Act calm. Act calm.

"Y-Yes. Yes." That was all I could say.

"I'm glad we agree." She laughed.

"Let's get going, Atlas," Mom said.

"Ok." Then I did it. I was brave. The bold strength that I'd felt in Celesteria during the Rephariamisi attack returned. My back straightened and I stared straight into Mom's blue eyes.

"Aamilah and I are going to practice," I looked at Mom then back at Aamilah. "Maybe she can come over to th-th-the house tomorrow?"

"That's fine with me, son. Ok with you Preston?" Mom turned to Dad. They were both standing at the end of the table.

"Sure," he answered, "but no goofing off. You want to win, Atlas. Whatever you do in life, you have to be in it to win it."

Everyone walked out of the room, except me. I floated. I was happier than I'd been since well before Charlie died. We passed the lockers on our way to the exit. I don't remember what anyone said, myself included. I practically skipped. Things were getting better every minute.

Then, just before we walked out, Miss Pendleton handed Mom a piece of paper.

"He's in room one seventeen, they moved him from Eastern Regional to the rehab center this morning."

"Thank you."

"See you tomorrow Atlas," Aamilah said as we stepped

off the curb. She turned to Miss Pendleton. "Can I call my dad to pick me up?"

"Ok. S-S-See you," I replied.

I followed Mom and Dad to the car.

"Mom?" I said as she opened the door.

"Yes?"

"Who's in room one seventeen at the rehab center?"

Dad was already behind the wheel, revving the engine. He should have been a racecar driver.

"That boy who was beat up by his drunk uncle. Your classmate, Harold Randolph." Mom joined Dad in the front of the car. "Come on," she said as I lingered beside the back door. "Get in, we're going to pay your friend a visit."

CHAPTER 40

"He's not my fr-fr-friend."

"What did you say, Atlas, dear?" Mom asked.

"Big Harold. He's n-n-n-not my friend."

"What?" Mom nudged Dad's shoulder. "Turn down the radio Preston, I can't hear your son."

"He's not my friend!" I shouted, just as Dad turned the radio off. The volume of my voice scared me nearly as much as what I said shocked Mom.

"What do you mean, Atlas? He's been in your class for a long time. I know that Wyatt is your buddy, but aren't you friends with the other guys?" Mom poked her face around the headrest and stared at me.

I squirmed in my seat.

"Well?" Mom asked.

"He's not my friend. He's r-r-really more like an enemy," I finally answered.

"Atlas Michael Forman. I am very surprised by you. Why is he your enemy? Why do you have any enemies? You're twelve years old!"

"Yes, Atlas, you should get along with people. You never know when you might find a business opportunity," Dad chimed in as he braked behind a large tractor and its orange triangle.

"Darn red lights," he muttered.

"I d-d-don't know why you are so con-con-concerned," I replied to Mom. "I'm fine with Wyatt and I get along with most everybody else. I don't know why we have to visit Big Harold."

"Because he's a human being, Atlas. He's a boy with no family. No friends, apparently," she scowled at me and rubbed the back of her neck.

"We got in a f-f-fight on the bus. He took my n-n-note from Charlie."

"A fight!" Mom. Her eyes darkened. "A note from Charlie?"

"Yes. Look Mom, Harold is a b-b-b-bully. He picks on everyone, ok? He's not a nice k-k-k-kid and I don't know why you want to go visit h-h-him in the ho-ho-hoospital."

"Because your mother cares about others," Dad answered.

"And, we care about people who don't have anyone to care for them, Atlas. Harold is all alone," Mom added.

"Well, I've been alone plenty –"

"Watch what you say," Dad cut me off. "You have more than most kids. If you want to go around feeling sorry for yourself, that's your issue. Not Harold's. Not mine. Not even Mom's."

"Easy, Preston," Mom said. "I *am worried* if you feel alone, Atlas. You're my son. *Our only son*." She looked at Dad.

"Yes, Atlas, we love you. But, we're going to visit this boy. So, deal with it," Dad said as he glared at me in the rearview mirror.

I looked away. I studied my folded hands in my lap. They were trembling a little.

"Are we clear?" Dad's harsh voice cut through the silence.

"Yes," I mumbled without looking up. I said nothing the rest of the way. The thoughts of what Big Harold did to me and Wyatt and lots of other kids only made me fume more and more as I sat in the back of the car, staring out the window.

Apparently, my resistance to this trip was a trivial matter for my parents. Mom and her anti-alcohol crusade ran roughshod over my feelings. And Dad was so bent on appeasing Mom, the progress I'd made by doing well in spelling bee practice might have just been undone.

As we drove along, Mom peppered Dad with questions about Harold's situation.

"What's going to happen to him? Is his mother even around? Is Social Services getting involved?"

"One at a time, dear," Dad sputtered. "I don't know. All I know is what the guys were saying at the courthouse this morning. Harold's uncle is in custody until the trial. He was in violation of his probation, on top of everything else."

"What does that mean for Harold?"

"Like I said, Meredith," Dad lowered his voice. "I don't know. I don't know anything about his family situation."

Mom huffed and crossed her arms.

"Just because I'm a lawyer, doesn't mean I know everything," Dad said.

The sky darkened as we crossed the railroad tracks a couple of miles from the rehab center.

"Looks like a thunderstorm's coming," Dad said. He whistled as he leaned over the steering wheel and stared through the windshield.

"I'm sorry, Preston," Mom said. "I'm not mad at you, just mad at the situation. And, especially mad at alcohol."

"I understand. But it's not alcohol's fault. It's the people who don't exercise self-control."

"Careful, Preston," Mom warned. "Charlie's gone because of alcohol."

I noticed the mirage-like reflection of Mom's

brochures in the windshield. Dad did too. He must have realized he was picking a fight he couldn't win because he didn't reply. Instead, he turned on the radio and drummed the steering wheel until we reached the rehab center.

"Ok," he said as he parked the car. "We're here."

As he pushed the shifter into park, splats of rain hit the windshield. Big fat drops crashed into the roof of the car and before I'd unbuckled my seatbelt, a volley of thunder roared overhead. Howling wind whipped around the car, spraying sheets of rain.

"Wow," Mom said, looking out the window. "That's a storm."

"It's squalling for sure," Dad said. He hooked his arm over the top of the front seat and looked back at me.

"What do you think Atlas? Want to go for it or sit here until it passes?"

"I don't care," I replied.

I looked out the window. The sky was an endless stretch of smoky pewter. A lightning bolt crackled to the ground just beyond the big roadside sign for Old George's Ribs and Pot Pies. Another one stung the middle of the woods to the left of the rehab center. Just as I looked at Dad to answer his question, a wave of red light – the glow – washed over the horizon.

"Did you see that?" Mom asked.

"You saw it?" I asked. I grabbed her headrest and pulled my face up to hers.

"You saw it, Mom?" I asked again. "The red light? In the sky? You saw it, right?" I jerked on the back of the headrest, jostling her pretty good.

"Calm down, Atlas," she said. She patted her hair. "Relax, ok? Yes, I saw the sky get all red for a second. Must be some kind of strange lightning strike."

"I didn't see anything," Dad said.

"Mom, it's not just a strange lightning st-st-strike. I've seen it during the middle of the d-d-day, and late at night. I've seen it a bunch. First time was at Ch-Charlie's funeral." I looked at my bright white fingernails. My hands were squeezing Mom's headrest so viciously, the ends of my fingernails were practically glowing. I relaxed my grip and scooted back into my seat.

"You know what? Let's go on in," I said.

"Hold on a second, mister. You can't just tell us you've been seeing red lights in the sky and then change the subject," Mom said. She turned in her seat and looked back. She and Dad were both staring at me, their rounded eyebrows arched like the hives in Celesteria.

"Well, I have seen it a few times," I answered. "Maybe it's just some of the stuff going on at the coal mines."

"I don't think so," Mom said. "There's more going on than you're saying, Mister."

"Hey look, the storm passed," I said and pointed out the window.

"Well, I'll be darned. That was a quick thunder

boomer," Dad replied.

We all looked out our windows. The sky was still angry and the sun was hidden behind a thick black sponge of clouds, but the rain was just trickling.

"It might be now or never," Dad said. He pointed out Mom's side of the car. "Looks like a gully-washer is headed this way."

A wall of rain was mowing across the open space between the rest of the town and our car.

"Let's do it." I opened my door and jumped out, both feet landing in a huge puddle.

"Yuck!" I exclaimed as I felt pellets of dirty water penetrate my shirt. My socks suddenly felt clammy and my shoes several pounds heavier. I looked down.

"Look before you leap," I whispered. The washtub-sized pothole swallowed my feet up past my ankles.

Mom tiptoed out of the car and onto the sidewalk. She looked back at me and laughed.

"Remind me to come back here and use that spot when we are bobbing for apples at Halloween," she said.

I lifted my feet out and followed her to the front door of the rehab center.

Squish, squish, went my shoes.

"I guess we don't have to ask where you are. We can just hear you coming or going." Dad said as he joined us near the automatic sliding doors under the white and blue illuminated sign:

Pinesburg Rehabilitation and Convalescence Entrance

"This is the place," Mom said. She led us across the cold tile toward the check in area.

Squish, squish, with every step.

Several sets of cataract-clouded eyes squinted at me with disapproval. A small cadre of elderly people sat in the dull flower-patterned chairs, reading old copies of *Prevention* and *Home & Garden*. A stack of wrinkled *Consumer Reports* sat in a wicker basket by the entrance to the waiting area.

A balding man in the corner, who was just coming up for air after being doubled over by a rat-a-tat of hacking coughs, expressed the sickly group's sentiments.

"Dumb teenagers, ain't smart enough to get out of the rain," I heard him say.

Squish. Squish.

I finally got to stop walking – and squishing – as we reached our destination. Mom leaned on the smooth countertop littered with brochures about everything from emphysema to rheumatoid arthritis. Near a frosted glass divider, behind a vanilla ice cream-colored sign with blueberry-colored stenciling *Receptionist*, sat a tender-eyed candy striper with a syrupy voice and a syrupy name.

"Hello, I'm Delilah," she purred. "Welcome to Pinesburg Rehabilitation and Convalescence Center."

"Hello, Delilah," Mom replied. "We're here to visit Harold Randolph. I believe," she scanned the paper from Miss Pendleton, "he is in room one seventeen."

"Are you family?" she asked.

"No, no we're not."

"Friends, then?" Delilah looked at me.

I looked down and fumbled with the batch of papers about privacy rights and medical history disclosure.

"Yes," Dad answered for me. He nudged me in the back. I lifted my head and stared at Delilah like a frog in a full moon.

She smiled. The unexpected sight of gleaming metal brackets and colored rubber bands married to her teeth caused me to flinch. I managed to grin back.

"We only allow two visitors at a time," she said and pulled a clipboard out from under her desktop. She slid it toward Mom.

"Please fill out the top half of this form and I'll need both adults to sign it."

"Why don't you and Atlas go in there?" Dad asked. "I can wait in the lobby and make some calls."

"You and M-M-Mom can g-g-g-go," I mumbled.

"No," Mom replied. She grabbed the chain pen from the counter and started writing. "He's your friend, Atlas."

"It's really sweet of you to come," Delilah said. "He hasn't had any visitors since he got here this morning." She leaned forward and whispered: "Most of the kids always have *someone* come with them when they are transferred from the hospital."

I gulped. I was about to speak when a flash of green caught my eye. I looked past Delilah's triple-pierced ear, just beyond a streak of orange hair adrift in a sea of peroxide-blonde. I saw the green flash again, above the rows of manila file folders.

"Ok," Delilah said, taking the clipboard from Mom. "Here are your name tags." She handed us a couple stickers and a black Sharpie. "Write your first and last name on these, wear them at all times. You have thirty minutes to visit the patient."

CHAPTER 41

Harold's room was double occupancy. Fortunately, he was in the first bay, so we didn't have to walk past the kidney stone victim in the other bed. Hearing him wail was enough to make me jot a mental note: *drink more water*.

A symphony of digital beeps and electronic gongs welcomed us. Several monitors framed the head of Harold's bed. Black squares with highlighter green squiggly lines ricocheted to and fro.

Harold's pudgy face was black and blue and rounder than I'd remembered. Mom clapped her hand over her mouth. Tears formed in the corner of her eyes.

Squish. Squish.

Mom glared at me.

"Sorry," I mouthed.

Both of Harold's arms had gauze-wound boards holding IVs in place. He didn't stir when we walked in. Mom and I didn't move once we reached the end of his bed. For a while, we just stood there and held our breath.

The odor of antiseptics and the chilled air made my stomach turn. I hugged myself and rubbed my arms to create some heat.

Mom tiptoed toward the middle of Harold's bed. He didn't budge. His stomach rose and fell slowly, deliberately. An occasional shudder overcame his body when his breath was slow in coming.

"Atlas, this poor boy," Mom whispered. She held her fist to the spot just under the end of her nose and sniffed. "Poor boy, poor, poor boy," she muttered over and over.

"Mom, my stomach hurts," I whispered. "Can I go to the bathroom?"

Mom flicked her hand at me to go.

I looked at the chestnut-colored handicap-accessible door in the wall behind me. The black label with gold lettering, *Restroom*.

I heard another groan from bay number two, just on the other side of the curtain. I put my hands in my pocket.

Not in Mr. Kidney Stone's bathroom, I thought.

I walked out into the hallway.

Squish. Squish.

I looked to my left and saw nothing but dreary tile

floor awash in pale fluorescence.

I turned to my right. I spotted the public restrooms down the hall. Under a flickering ceiling light panel in desperate need of a replacement bulb, I noticed the cut out in the wall and the pimple of a sign that popped out about two-thirds of the way up.

Squish. Squish. Squish.

As I walked past open rooms with blaring televisions and bleary-eyed nurses, I thought back to the nights at the hospital, hoping Charlie would recover.

"Man, hospitals suck," I said as I ducked into the bathroom.

After turning the privacy corner and nearly tripping over a yellow plastic tent, warning me in English and Spanish of a slippery surface, I gathered myself and looked to the right. The shallow porcelain urinals were empty, except for their bright blue disinfecting biscuits.

I leaned down a bit. No feet under the stalls. I didn't have to use the bathroom; I just didn't want to stay in Harold's room.

The gallery of sinks was my first stop. Four deep ceramic squares, centered under shoebox-sized mirrors. After turning on the faucet in sink number two, I hunched over and cupped the cool water in my hands, watching it bubble over and through my fingers.

It spilled and refilled in my hand, over and over. Finally, I splashed a double handful against my face. I looked in the mirror and smiled as beads rolled down my cheeks and chin, dripping into the basin.

It felt good. As I cupped my hands for a second round, a green flash behind me reflected in the mirror.

I stood up straight and wiped my hands on my pants as I turned to locate it.

"Where are you?" I asked.

"Right here," Talia popped over the door of stall number one. "Come here," she said as she dropped behind the door.

I walked over and opened the stall door.

"Come in, close the door behind you."

I pulled the door shut behind me and clicked the latch. In front of me was a toilet. Hovering at eye level was Talia, resplendent in a robin's egg blue cloak, trimmed in ivory lace.

Instinctively, my hand reached out. She floated onto it. The sensation caused by her touch rippled through my skin. Her freckles practically danced along her cheeks as she began to speak.

"I have no time for pleasantries. I have no time for anything save one thing - saving Harold, my Renall Benji. He is running out of time."

My eyes widened. A large drop of water fell from my hairline onto my hand, spraying Talia.

"I'm sorry, I-I-I…"

She smoothed her ornate cloak and didn't miss a beat.

"The soul can only stand and believe for so long without support. Without reinforcement. The body is a muted reflection of the soul. Many assault the body in order to defeat the soul."

"What does th-th-that mean?"

"It means that more than Harold's physical health hangs in the balance. His very essence is nearly gone. His power is fading. His desire to dream and his ability to hope has been under a relentless attack since before he was born. I have labored too long and too deliberately to see his flame snuffed out."

"B-B-But, I," I tried to reply.

Talia raised her hand.

"Just listen, Atlas. Should the sun set on his hardening heart, it will forever be stone. I have engaged you at great peril. But, desperation drives destiny. And you alone can bring Harold's destiny back to life."

"I d-d-d-don't understand. Harold h-h-hates me."

"Hate," Talia repeated. She crossed her arms and bobbed into the air, leaving my hand. She drifted to my face and paralyzed me with her arctic stare. Her blue eyes stunned me to silence.

"You don't know hate. You use words without thinking, like most humans, like words are disposable. Like they don't have consequences. Like they don't *create* consequences.

"Sorry," I said.

"Hate is a vacuum, a void. It is anti-matter. It is darkness without light. It is the absence of love, and the absence of compassion. Before hate comes suspicion. Before suspicion comes ignorance. You and Harold don't hate each other. You don't *know* each other."

She moved down to my chest and pressed her hands against my heart.

"You *know* of each other. But you don't know each other. *Here.* In your hearts. Where it counts. Forgiveness is the fire in which friendship is forged."

A clattering sound followed by a grunt interrupted our conversation.

"Stupid wet floor sign," I heard a deep voice mutter.

"What am I supposed to-to-to do?" I whispered to Talia.

"Atlas? Is that you?" It was Dad. "Hang on a second, Winston. Actually, let me call you back."

I heard a snap of plastic as Dad closed his old cell phone, then a tap on the stall door.

"You in there, Atlas?"

"Yes Dad."

"Who were you talking to?"

"No one. I was j-ju-just th-th-thinking out loud."

Talia drifted away from my chest. She hovered for a couple seconds, pressing her hands against her chest. She pointed at my heart and mouthed, "Forgive."

"How's Harold look?" Dad asked.

280

Talia spun into a green flash. She was gone.

I leaned against the inside of the stall and stared at the polished metal piping, the white bowl. I reached over and flushed, watching the cyclone of water swirl until it disappeared.

I opened the door.

Dad was at the sink, washing his hands. He made eye contact with me in the mirror.

"Is Harold in rough shape?"

"Yes, Dad," I said. "He doesn't look very good at all."

Dad shook the excess water from his hands and grabbed a clump of paper towels from the metal shelving under the mirror. He turned around and dried his hands as he spoke.

"I was on the phone with Winston Barnes over at Social Services. Harold doesn't have *anybody*. His dad got locked up last week for armed robbery, which means he's out of the picture, and his mom hasn't been heard from in like a decade. No grandparents, either. The uncle charged with beating him was the last of Harold's relatives."

Dad put his arm around my shoulder. We walked out of the bathroom, careful not to trip on the wet floor sign.

Squish, squish.

"We are a blessed family, Atlas."

"Yes," I agreed.

We walked to Harold's room.

"Let's get Mom and head on home," Dad said as I

walked through the doorway. "Meemaw is probably running out of patience with Hannah."

We both stopped just inside the door and stared at the ground beside Harold's bed. There, on the floor, was Mom. She was on her knees, with her chin on the plastic bar that ran along the top of the mattress. Her hands were atop Harold's.

"Meredith?" Dad asked finally. "Are you ok?"

Harold's eyes fluttered. He groaned and rolled his head back and forth against his pillow.

"Harold?" Mom whispered. She stood to her feet and stepped to the top of the bed. She leaned down to Harold's face.

"Harold? Can you hear me?"

His cracked lips stuck together, but he moved them enough to allow a feeble "yea" to pass.

"Atlas," Mom turned to me. Tear tracks lined her face. Her red and shiny nose looked like a fruit punch lollipop stuck below her bloodshot eyes.

"Come talk to your friend," she said.

Squish, squish.

I walked over to Harold's bed and held up my hand in a half-wave.

"Hey H-H-Harold," I said.

He turned his head to my voice. His bruised and swollen face turned red as he strained to open his eyes. Finally, he was able to focus his eyes in my direction.

"Hey," he whispered.

Mom moved behind me.

"Come here, honey," I heard Dad say.

Harold held his eyes open. They were nearly blank. The word that came to mind was *weary*. Like he'd been climbing uphill his whole life and still hadn't glimpsed a single mountain peak.

"I'm s-s-sorry Harold," I mumbled.

His eyes flickered. Like a car engine trying to start, they blinked and flashed, then went blank again.

"I m-m-mean it," I said. Hot tears rolled down my cheek and dripped onto the thin sheet covering Harold.

"I'm so s-s-s-sorry, H-H-Harold."

His eyes blinked again. Once, twice, three times. This time, they didn't go blank. They stayed. He looked at me. Eye to eye. Heart to heart.

"Me too," he whispered. His voice was hoarse and dry, but it was clear.

Melting snow.

That's what it felt like, from the space between us, through our skin and bones, to our soul. Like Talia said, forgiveness set a fire that burned away all the ice and anger that was caked on from years of misunderstanding, rudeness and rage.

"Atlas," Harold creaked, "thank you." He closed his eyes. His lips turned up, just a little, just enough.

I turned to Mom and Dad. They were watching.

Smiling.

They held out their arms and I walked into their embrace.

"You're right Dad," I said. "We are a blessed family."

CHAPTER 42

When we got home from the rehab center, Meemaw, Hannah, and Wyatt were at the kitchen table, playing cards.

"Where y'all been?" Meemaw looked up at us before turning to Wyatt with a smirk, "Go fish, young man."

Wyatt plucked the top card from the stack in the middle of the table. He looked up at me and smiled.

"I called and y'all weren't home, so Meemaw told me to just come on over."

"Cool," I answered.

"And look at this," Wyatt said, holding up a rock.

The Harpazzo stone, I thought for a second.

"Where'd you get that?" I asked excitedly.

"Calm down, buddy," Wyatt replied. He looked across

the table at Meemaw. "She found it for me. I must have left it here the night of Charlie's funeral."

"Yep," Meemaw added. "I was cleaning behind the sofa in the front room, and I found that rock. I almost threw it out but the pretty colors made me think it might be something worth hanging onto. Then Wyatt saw it and said he thought it'd been stolen."

"I guess you owe Harold an apology," I interrupted.

Wyatt hung his head. Then he smiled. "I suppose so."

"Hey everybody," Hannah grinned.

Dad scooped Hannah up from the table and held her aloft. He tickled her tummy with his nose, causing her to laugh and spill her cards all over the floor.

"Hey, there's that eight I need to make my set," Meemaw said. "Guess that's the end of the game."

"Want to go upstairs, Atlas?" Wyatt asked. He stood and placed his cards on the stack. "Thank you Meemaw."

She stood and dropped her cards beside his. "You're welcome young man. And you're welcome here anytime."

"Who's hungry?" Mom asked.

"Me!" a chorus of voices answered.

Hannah raised her hand and said, "Me too!"

"How about spaghetti and meatballs?" Mom asked, pulling open the pantry door.

"Sounds good to me, dear," Dad replied.

"Great," Meemaw added.

"You staying for dinner Wyatt?" Mom asked.

"Yes ma'am, if that's allright?"

"Of course."

I followed Wyatt out of the kitchen. We walked up the stairs together and entered my room. I pulled the door shut behind us. This time, I made sure it was locked.

"So, where's the case?" Wyatt asked. He plopped into my desk chair and spun around. As he twirled faster and faster, he laughed.

"I'll get it," I said.

Please open, I thought while walking to my bed. I reached under my pillow and felt nothing. I drove my hands deeper. Still nothing. I ripped the covers off my bed and tossed the pillow over my shoulder, scratching at the mattress, tugging and fighting for something to appear. Nothing.

I dropped to the ground and tunneled under the bed. The floor was bare except for the dusty old candy. I slid out and bumped into Wyatt. He was standing beside my bed.

"What happened?" he asked.

I stood beside him and folded my hands atop my head.

"I don't know. It was there, it was just there," I pointed at my bed. "I swear, I swear, it's real. It was there."

"Easy, Atlas. I'm sure it's here, somewhere. It's not like this place is very clean. It could have gotten misplaced, right?" Wyatt tugged at his cap and looked around the room.

"No, no, no. I p-p-put it under m-m-my p-pil-pillow."

"Well, let's just look around. Try to calm down, buddy," Wyatt said.

"Calm down!" I shouted. "I c-c-c-can't. You d-d-d-don't under-st-st-stand."

Wyatt froze.

"What's that?" He pointed at the top of my bookshelf. I followed his finger with my line of sight.

A green flash darted across the wall.

"Talia," I said. My heart jumped. "She's here!"

"What? Who?" Wyatt asked, still frozen.

Just like that, Talia was hovering before us.

"Hello Atlas," she said, nodding her head in a half-bow. "I came one last time to thank you. Harold is on the rise." She held out her hands. A tightly wrapped scroll appeared, tied with a green ribbon.

"What the…" Wyatt's jaw hung wide as he stammered in disbelief.

I smiled. "This, my good friend Wyatt, is Talia." I waved in her direction. "Who is also my good friend."

She winked. "My time is short gentlemen. Wyatt, believe me, you need to believe Atlas. More important, the day will come when you must believe in Atlas."

Wyatt blinked. He didn't speak.

"At least close your mouth." I laughed. "You don't want to catch flies."

"Again, Atlas, thank you." Talia held out the scroll.

"But, Talia," I said. "Where's the case? The stone? The book?"

"It is gone for now, Atlas."

"But, but…"

"For now. As you have learned, your interaction with Celesteria was premature. But, remember, nothing is accidental. Anything is possible."

"But, but, the book. My note…"

"I believe this will alleviate your fears." She pushed the scroll into my hands.

"Anything is possible." She spun into the green flash and she was gone.

I looked down at the scroll. It was rolled so tightly it was as hard as a pencil, and almost as long.

"Wha, what, what was that?" Wyatt asked.

"Now, you're the one with the st-st-stutter," I replied.

"Well, uh, yeah."

"Wyatt, it's real. Celesteria is real. Talia is a creature from there. They are like our protectors. I guess kinda like angels. She is Big Harold's guardian. Or, the guardian of Big Harold's dreams."

I sat down on the bed.

Wyatt sat down beside me. He leaned back against the wall, shaking his head slowly.

"I never. I never would have believed it. But, I saw it. I saw it, right?" he asked, sitting up straight.

"Yep." I nodded.

"Well, are you going to read it?" Wyatt pointed at the scroll.

"I guess I should, huh?"

I pulled at the ribbon. It gave way easily and drifted toward my lap. As it fell, it melted, like evaporation. Before reaching my lap, it was gone.

"Whoa," Wyatt shook his head again.

I unrolled the scroll. As soon as the brittle paper was unpeeled, I recognized the writing.

"What? What is it?" Wyatt asked.

I didn't reply. It was Charlie's note. Except it was different. It was finished. As I read it silently, the tears returned. The first time I'd read Charlie's note, they were tears of sorrow. This time, they were tears of joy.

Dear Atlas,

I ben itching to tell you some things latly. You have a lot of dreams. They are cool. I wished I was smart like you. I don't always appreskiate what you like. I don't always ~~understand~~

~~figure out~~   ~~know how to say~~

Coach Jefferson said something last week and I can't hardly get it out my brains. He said we got to never change what we was made to be, no matter what othur people think.

I see you all   the time playing alone, and I know you feel kinda diffrent. I think you should just be yourself, because nobody will ever understand everything in the world the same way you do.

You must be yourself. It is more important than you can know. It is everthing. So, keep heart. Don't give up. Time tells all. In time, you will see all.

Love,
Charlie

P.S. Marty says hello.

"Atlas! Wyatt! Time for spaghetti and meatballs!"

The lump in my throat wasn't ready to make room for spaghetti, much less a meatball.

I looked at Wyatt.

He was shaking his head. Blonde hairs popped straight up like a thousand tiny blades of grass on his arms.

I nodded.

"Come on boys, dinner time!"

"Ok," Wyatt whispered.

"I don't think she heard you," I whispered back.

We both smiled, then started laughing. We stood up and I rolled the note and picked up the picture of the fishing trip with Marty and Charlie from my bookshelf.

I stared at the picture for a minute. The smiles were real. For a moment, it almost felt like we were all together again.

I held it with the scroll and tucked them both in the top drawer of my desk. I slid the door closed and turned to Wyatt.

"Now do you believe me?" I asked, reassuring myself as the words left my mouth.

He gulped and nodded his head.

"I'll take that as a yes," I said.

"Yes," he said. "Definitely a yes." His senses slowly returned. "I've got so many questions. What is Talia? Where is Celesteria? How did you get there?"

"Atlas! Wyatt! Come on boys!"

"Coming Mom!" I yelled.

I turned to Wyatt once more.

"I'll tell you everything I know," I said. "It's not much and it's not close to complete. I think it's like Talia says. It's not our time yet."

"I guess," Wyatt replied.

"Let's go eat some spaghetti," I said. "Race ya!"

I bolted out of the room and bounded down the stairs three at a time. Wyatt trailed behind, unable to overcome my surprise head start.

I ran into the kitchen, only to find it empty.

"We're in here, Atlas," Dad called from the dining room.

I walked into the adjoining room and sniffed the air. The smell of tomato paste and basil and Parmesan cheese got my stomach growling. Everyone was seated around the table, with Mom's china neatly placed in front of every seat.

"Thought it was time we started living again," Mom said.

"Some of us never stopped," Meemaw whispered to Hannah, who was clutching a handful of playing cards.

"Go fish," Hannah whispered back.

"Smells great Mrs. Forman," Wyatt said from behind me.

"Don't just stand there, boys, take a seat," Dad said.

The food was delicious. We ate 'til we nearly burst. Everyone chatted freely, talking about school getting out soon, if Hannah would be old enough to go to swim camp, and whether I would win the spelling bee in three weeks.

"I reckon you can do it," Wyatt said.

"He's got a study helper coming over tomorrow," Mom smiled.

"Who is it?" Meemaw asked.

"Aamilah." Mom smiled even bigger.

"That foreign girl I drove to school the other day?" Meemaw asked. "Isn't her dad the new doctor no one will visit?"

"Yes," I answered.

"Uh-hum," Meemaw said. "Someone pass me the rolls."

"I don't know how you can eat anymore," Dad said, handing Meemaw the straw woven basket draped with a linen napkin, filled with warm hunks of bread.

"Mind your manners, young fella," Meemaw said.

"Excuse me," Mom said. "I'll be back in two shakes." She pushed her chair back and walked into the kitchen.

She returned carrying a plastic tray of cupcakes.

"Where'd you get those?" Dad asked.

"A lady never tells," Mom replied. She walked around the table dropping one on the edge of each person's plate.

"Duck. Duck. Duck," Mom said, until reaching her seat.

"Goose!" she laughed and put two cupcakes on her plate.

"Nice, Meredith," Dad said.

"I like your style, Mrs. Forman," Wyatt added.

"Enjoy everybody," Mom said.

We did enjoy it. Every bite. Mouths full of moist chocolate cake, lips ringed with rich fudge icing. I was about three bites deep when Dad spoke up from the other end of the table.

"Atlas, Mom and I have something we want to ask you."

I looked up. Unable to speak or even mumble, I nodded.

"Atlas," Mom said. "You know your friend in the rehab center, Harold?"

"Meth," I said through a half-swallowed chunk of cupcake.

"Well," Dad interjected, "you know I talked to Winston Barnes at Social Services. And Harold has literally no family. No one to visit him, no one to take care of him, no one to go home to. Nothing."

"And, honey," Mom said, "when I was in his room today, my heart just broke. The poor boy has nothing, and when he gets better, he's going to get sent to some foster home or worse, a group home. He'll probably have to go to a new school, make new friends, all that, unless…"

"Unless," Dad finished for her, "someone offers to take him in."

"What we're getting at, Atlas is this. Why not us?

Why don't we take Harold in?" Mom asked. "We've got the room."

Wyatt looked at me across the table. I knew what he was thinking. It's what I was thinking.

Big Harold. Living in my house!

I looked down at my plate and pushed my cupcake away.

"You don't have to decide right now," Mom said.

All I could think of was Talia's words about forgiveness, and friendship. All I could hear in my mind was her plea to help Big Harold. All I could see was his bruised body, his full-force effort just to open his eyes in the bed.

Hannah clapped her hands.

I looked at her soft green eyes across the table. Her little arms stretched over her plate, her cheeks and chin were smudged with frosting.

I stood up.

"Sorry Atlas, we weren't trying to upset you," Mom said.

I looked at Wyatt and nodded as I circled to Hannah's seat.

"But, the sooner we can tell Winston Barnes…" Dad said.

Hannah reached up and we gave each other a big hug, her chocolate fingers certainly smearing the back of my shirt.

"It's ok," I finally answered. "Yeah. It's fine. He can

stay with us." I stood back from Hannah's seat and looked around the table.

Wyatt's eyes nearly popped out of his head.

Mom clutched her hands to her chest.

Dad smiled.

"You know, I'm so glad, Atlas," Mom said. "Nothing happens by accident."

Just over Mom's shoulder, a flash of green flitted across the wall and disappeared. I'm pretty sure I saw a red glow through the window in the fading daylight.

"Yes. Nothing is accidental, Mom." I smiled as I spoke clear and easy, my stutter a world away.

"And anything is possible."